SABER

DRAGON BRIDES

KATE RUDOLPH

ABOUT SABER

The betrothal is bad.

Prince Saber regrets agreeing to an arranged marriage the moment he says yes. His bride is a dull aristocratic lady who he'll be bound to for the rest of his life. No fated mate. No adventure. No love. So when he's given an off planet mission he accepts it in a heartbeat. He can't escape the betrothal, but he can delay it.

The ship crash? That's a disaster.

Lady Mirage needs to talk to her betrothed. Alone. What better place than a space ship? But he's not supposed to take off before he realizes she's on board. When she and her betrothed crash land on a barren planet, they'll need to rely on each other to survive. But that's not the only trouble. There's a dangerous fugitive on the planet with them ready to attack.

Mirage is tougher than she looks, and it's not long before she and Saber are finding they fit together in more ways than one. But she has a secret. A big one. Will he still want her when he finds out the truth?

Fated mates, fierce women, and dragon princes are ready to find their mates in the new Dragon Brides series from Kate Rudolph.

Saber passed by the matchmaker's shop and continued down the block. His father's most recent demand was ringing in his head, but he couldn't just say yes.

Not even to make him proud.

Finally.

It was hard being the youngest son of the king. Some days it seemed all he could do was screw up.

He turned the corner, and when he had the choice to head back towards the palace, he went the other way and circled the block, passing in front of the matchmaker another time.

She was supposed to be psychic. That was what they whispered through the city. And if she was psychic, maybe she could tell him if he was about to make a muck of this. He didn't want to tie himself to someone he could never love.

But it wasn't like he was knocking away prospects left and right. Dragon women wanted the heir, not the youngest son.

He passed by the matchmaker and circled the block again.

He should just go home. If Crux or Ranger heard what he was thinking, they'd both think he was crazy. He wouldn't hear the end of it. And they teased him enough as it was.

But why would they know?

He wasn't going to tell them.

When he got near the shop a third time, the door was open.

"Make up your mind, your highness. You're scaring clients away," came a voice from inside the storefront.

Saber jolted. He didn't realize he was that obvious. And he almost kept walking. Who was this matchmaker to order a prince? He didn't care that it said *Royal Matchmaker* on her window. There was nothing royal about her.

But he went inside anyway.

He wasn't sure what he expected. Not a cozy little room with a nice sofa, a fireplace, and two chairs. It looked more like a sitting room than a business.

Saber looked at the woman, the Royal

Matchmaker, and wasn't sure what to think of her. She was middle aged, with dark hair, light brown skin, and bright blue eyes. She looked him up and down in turn.

"How did you know who I was?" He knew the question was ridiculous as soon as it left his mouth.

The matchmaker smiled. "You are the prince, sir. Your face is quite well known."

It was the truth. And it made privacy an issue. But he wasn't about to complain about that. "Do you have a name?"

She slid a small card his way. It read: SHADE | ROYAL MATCHMAKER.

"Take a seat, your highness." Shade gestured at the couches. "Would you like tea? Or perhaps a snack? I just bought a box of cookies from the baker up the road."

It was tempting, but Saber was on his guard. He didn't know this woman, and he wasn't about to accept food from a stranger. "I'm alright."

She shrugged and took a seat before he could. Saber was left standing. He could walk right out and forget this had ever happened. Instead he sat on the couch.

"Tell me your troubles." Shade made it a demand, and for some reason, he wanted to comply. When his father ordered him to do things, he bristled.

He slumped a little and let his worries out. "I'm

supposed to agree to an arranged marriage. I don't know if it's the right choice. I always thought I'd..." he trailed off. It was too embarrassing to say out loud, especially since he was a prince.

"I keep everything in the strictest confidence," Shade assured him, leaning in. "Please, be honest."

Who was she going to tell? And why would they believe her? "I always wanted to find my mate." It came out in a rush, and he could feel his cheeks pinking. "If I agree to an arrangement, I'm giving that up."

Shade hummed and leaned back in her chair. She was silent for several moments, and Saber wondered if he was supposed to speak. Then she nodded to herself and leaned forward once more. "Your concerns are well considered. A mate is a blessing few are fortunate enough to find. But your fate is waiting for you... if you are brave enough to see it. Have faith."

He waited for her to say more.

She didn't.

"Is that it?" She was supposed to be psychic. Anyone on the street could have said something like that.

At least he wasn't paying her.

Shade shrugged and crossed her legs, casually running her fingers over the seam of her chair. "I'm not about to select your bride, young man. Keep my words in mind. Now, unless you'd like a more in depth talk, it's time for you to leave."

And before Saber could fully comprehend what was happening, she'd urged him out of his seat and out the door.

He headed back down the block and turned towards the palace, but instead of going there, he turned towards the fields outside the city. He wanted to fly and he wanted privacy. It was too bad he couldn't escape to his cabin tonight.

He let his dragon form overtake him and sprang into the air, wings pumping and letting him fly free. He let out a small burst of fire in celebration of his flight. He loved to soar through the air and feel the wind under his wings.

There were mountains in the distance that he flew toward. There was no hope of making it all that way before he had to turn back, but he liked the idea of finding a perch and refusing to leave.

He'd flown for some time when a shadow overhead caught his attention.

A smaller, red female dragon joined him. She shot a playful burst of flame his way in greeting and flew close enough to him that he feared they'd collide in midair.

She was challenging him to a race.

She was doomed to failure.

Joy shot through Saber as they sped through the

sky. On the ground, several children watched them as they danced through the air. His companion was just as skilled a flyer as he was, and she impressed him with a few of her flips and rolls.

If they were on the ground, he might even ask her advice on how to improve his speed.

But their flight couldn't last forever. And after an hour or so, she split off from him and headed east.

He wished he knew who she was. He'd like to fly like that again.

Saber landed outside of the palace walls and headed towards his room before he could be found and summoned to his father. Back in his human form, the matchmaker's words rang in his head.

Your fate is waiting for you… if you are brave enough to see it.

Nonsense. Fated waited for no one. And he was more than brave. What did a person need to be brave enough to see?

She spoke nonsense, either to play mind games or for some even more sinister reason. Saber didn't like it. And he wouldn't be recommending her services to anyone.

In his quarters, he flopped down onto his mattress and contemplated his future. If he said yes to his father's command and married a suitable dragoness, he might actually earn a sliver of his father's favor.

If he said no, he'd continue to be a disappointment. Or worse, an afterthought.

He wouldn't be giving up anything real if he said yes. Just a chance at a mate, and that wasn't likely, anyway. So few found their own. Why did he think he was special?

So why did thinking *yes* make him feel like a failure?

He had time to make his decision. But Saber feared he already knew which way he'd go.

He only hoped he didn't live with regret for the rest of his life.

2

One Month Ago

Mirage sat at her dressing table and applied another coat of makeup. Her skin was already coated in the stuff, and she shimmered faintly when the light caught her just right. Would her betrothed be bothered when he discovered that she didn't actually sparkle? As if that was the harshest truth about her.

Would she be forced to fake a sparkle for the rest of her life?

She tried not to let the apprehension show on her face. She was about to meet her prince. This was what she'd been raised to do. And she was going to do her family proud by securing her man and raising their status in the kingdom.

What was her freedom compared to that?

"No need for a light touch with the brush. You

should shine." Her mother sat on the bench beside her and reached for a pot of makeup, holding it up to her face and matching the brown powder to Mirage's brown skin. "A bit more of this, I think. To cover up that mark. I want you to look like a true dragon."

Mirage turned away to hide her flinch. That mark was a small scar she'd received playing as a child. No one noticed it except for her mother, and it was already more than covered up. As for looking like a true dragon… well, there was nothing more Mirage could do about that. She looked how she looked, and she wasn't ashamed. "I doubt his highness will reject me because of it."

Her mother made an annoyed sound. "There's no use leaving this to chance. He can walk away until the dedication ceremony. You can't let him see your flaws. Not *a single one.*"

"And there are so many of those," Mirage muttered. Her fingers gripped her makeup brush tightly.

"What was that?" Her mother pushed the pot of makeup toward her.

Mirage grabbed it and placed it back on the table and the brush beside it. "Nothing, mother. But I think I'm painted enough. One day his highness will see me without makeup, and I don't want him to think I'm a stranger." She normally wore almost nothing on her face. It irritated her skin and made her sweat. And when she shifted, it all came off anyway.

Her mother laughed like it was a joke. "I'd birthed you and both of your brothers before your father saw my face bare. You'd be wise to do the same. You take after me."

"I certainly don't take after Father." Mirage couldn't hold the jab back.

It was her mother's turn to flinch. "Don't say things like that."

"You look fine." And she was right, Mirage did look like her mother: same brown skin, same dark, wavy hair, same green eyes. Mirage may as well have been her mother's clone. For looks alone, she didn't see anything wrong with that. In fact, it was pure luck and had probably saved her life at birth.

She hated hiding herself. All of herself. But her mother would never allow her to tell the whole truth. It would ruin them all.

"Now, remember, the prince should lead the conversation. Agree with what he says and don't speak over him. And do not say a word about your flying exploit. We wouldn't want him to think you're a thrill seeker."

"We're dragons. Flying is a vital part of our existence." Mirage could feel her wings trying to spread under her skin. She wanted to run away for a flight right now. But if she left, she'd probably never come back.

"You are a lady before you are a dragon, never forget that. The court won't. You must be above reproach. Don't talk about your time at university unless he indicates a love of education. And even then, don't let yourself seem smarter than him. And make sure you don't allow any liberties. He can't have you until the formalities are seen to."

"Mother!" Mirage couldn't believe what she was hearing. "You're being a hypocrite."

Her mother ignored her and blustered on. "Hmm, what am I forgetting?" She tapped her fingers against the table.

"Should I remain silent the whole time?" she asked tartly.

"Don't be ridiculous, darling. You should at least speak when prompted." Her mother stood and kissed the air above her hair, afraid to muss the carefully crafted style. "I've worked very hard for this match. I know you won't disappoint the family."

"We shouldn't do this." She wasn't supposed to say it. She knew her mother wouldn't hear it. But Mirage *had* to say something.

"Whyever not?" Her mother had the gall to look confused.

Mirage blinked several times, as if that would make her ears understand what she was hearing. She looked around the room, even though there was no reason to think they weren't alone. "Because he doesn't know the truth. He thinks that I'm—"

"You are exactly who we say you are." Her mother gripped her shoulder tightly. "Your dragon form is strong. Your fire burns hot and bright. You're as much a dragon lady as I am."

"Only half."

Silence hung in the air at her words. Some of the color drained from her mother's face, but if Mirage hadn't been looking, she would have missed it, her mother recovered so quickly. "You are the one who will carry the consequences if that comes to light. Make peace with it, dear. You can be a dragon princess. Or you can be nothing." She patted Mirage on the shoulder and left her to finish getting ready.

Mirage stared at her face and then contemplated the makeup powder her mother had insisted she add. No. She wasn't putting anything else on her face.

She knew no one could see that she was an interloper in the dragon world, a testament to her mother's own pre-marital folly. To all appearances, she was a true dragon, and she had never let the truth slip.

Could she live with herself if she went through with this? Could she survive if she didn't?

Her dress was hanging on the door to her dressing

room, a gold and green garment that perfectly set off her skin and eyes. She felt like a mannequin as she pulled it on and studied herself in the mirror. Mirage looked like the lady her mother wanted her to be, prim and dim and proper. The perfect match for the king's youngest son.

She would be a princess.

She shuddered.

All eyes would be on her all of the time. There would be no more sneaking off for flights to clear her head. No more walking down the streets with no one paying her any mind. No more privacy.

How could she do this?

Mirage breathed deep. She had to. Her mother had worked hard for this moment and she wasn't going to let her family down. This was what she was born for, and she was going to do it.

She held her shoulders high and glided out of the room to where her family was waiting. Her father and brothers made appreciative sounds when they saw her, and her mother looked her up and down and gave a satisfied nod.

She wasn't a failure yet, and their vehicle was waiting.

The ride to the palace went by in a blur. If her mother gave her more instructions, she wasn't listening.

Then Mirage was left alone again. But this part

she knew; she'd been talked through the ceremony plenty of times.

And she wasn't really alone. Courtiers lined the halls, watching as she made her way down the flower lined path to the throne room. King Venin sat on his throne while her betrothed, Prince Saber, stood beside him. His two older brothers, Prince Crux and Prince Ranger, stood behind the throne.

The flowers stopped several feet before the dais, and that was where Mirage was meant to end her walk. She bowed deep and held the position.

After a moment her calves and abs burned, but she couldn't stand until the king acknowledged her.

He only made her wait another moment.

"Lady Mirage, come and meet your betrothed," said the king, his benevolent voice booming out around her.

Mirage rose. Prince Saber wore a somber expression on his handsome face. She didn't think he was covered in a dozen layers of makeup, though there might have been a bit of liner around his eyes and a bit of color on his lips. He was tall and well muscled, with pale skin and blue eyes. She might have even looked twice at him if she passed him on the street, and she imagined he'd look good out of his dark clothes.

At least some of her marital duties would be no hardship.

He held out a hand, and Mirage stepped forward to take it. "Your highness." She curtsied as she got close.

"My lady." He kissed her hand.

And that was that. They were betrothed.

The crowd around them gave the appropriate cheer, and servants began to bring in the food and drinks that would top off the celebration. Prince Saber kept hold of her hand.

Mirage kept the smile pasted to her face.

He didn't say another word to her.

And, following her mother's instructions, Mirage kept her mouth shut.

This marriage was going to be a disaster.

3

Sweat poured down Saber's forehead and into his eyes, stinging him enough that he had to swipe it away. That left him open to a blow from his partner, who jabbed him in the side and darted away before he could retaliate.

He hated fighting in human form. If he had claws and his fire, his partner wouldn't stand a chance.

Of course, if his partner was in *his* warrior form, Saber would have been disemboweled.

The gong rang, signaling the end of the fight, and they broke apart, shaking hands and backing away to lick their wounds.

For the past month, Saber had thrown himself into his training, cursing the fact the kingdom was at peace. If there was some battle to go fight, maybe he could put off the wedding that kept creeping ever closer.

And if he died in battle, he'd never need to get married. It was always useful to look at the bright side.

Saber toweled off his sweat and winced at his own thought. He had no wish to die, and it was unkind to Lady Mirage. She'd done nothing wrong… except be the dragon chosen for him.

He could tell his father no. That was the other way out of this match. But Saber would rather face a thousand enemies than say anything to the king. He'd agreed to the betrothal, he had to live with it.

"Your highness, your father requests your presence." Yotar, a long-time servant of the king, stood at the edge of the training circle. He gave a slight bow when Saber noticed him and gestured back towards the palace.

"I'll be there shortly," he told the man, who swiftly walked away once the message was received. Yotar's white robe swirled around him, but somehow didn't trip him. It had been something that fascinated Saber when he was young, but now he just accepted it as a fact of the world.

Saber had been meeting with his father more and more in the past weeks, especially since he was the only brother reliably on the planet anymore. That meant Crux and Ranger were calling down the king's wrath, and it was almost a relief to not be the disappointment. For now. He quickly washed up and hurried through the palace halls, past the throne room, and to the chamber his father used as an office.

King Venin sat behind his desk and looked up when Saber entered. He wore a dark uniform with golden braiding on one shoulder and a discreet crown. The metal glinted in the light, but it wasn't encrusted in jewels like his more formal crowns. "Take a seat," he bade.

That wasn't bad. For a long time, Saber had been made to stand at attention while his father berated him. These days he was allowed to sit. And so he did. He was still wearing training clothes, and while his father did give him a withering look, he didn't openly critique them.

"The high priestess has suggested moving your dedication ceremony to the night of the next moon festival. I've given approval and notified Lady Mirage and her family. See that you are ready." The king spoke in a brusque manner as he always did with Saber.

That was far sooner than he'd anticipated. They were meant to be betrothed for at least a year. "What about Crux? Will he and his mate be back by then?" Saber didn't want to face marriage without both of his brothers there for support.

The king scowled. "He knows his time limit. And

he'll bring his *human* mate if he must." He said the word human like it tasted particularly foul. "I'm sure Ranger will bring *his* human as well. At least you'll continue the line with a proper dragon. Perhaps I'll upset them all and name you my heir. Will that set the three of you at war?" His father grinned at that disturbing prospect.

The only war would involve Saber doing his best not to be named king. That was a fate left to Crux, and Saber didn't want it. He was smart enough not to say it. "They have found their fated mates, surely that's a blessing."

The king huffed in disapproval.

Saber was jealous. He'd never tell his brothers such, but it seethed within him. They not only got to choose their brides, they'd found the women fate intended for them. While he was left with Lady Mirage, a woman he could barely speak two words to without his tongue tying in knots.

What was a man even supposed to *say* to a lady? Did she have interests? If she did, she was doing her best to hide them from him.

"Blessing or not, we are royal dragons. We have a duty." The king stared at him, daring him to challenge the statement. As if Saber would.

"Yes, sir." The kingdom had celebrated when Ranger presented his mate, Sidney, to the court. They didn't care that she was human. It was something that only seemed to matter to his father. But Saber kept his mouth shut.

Then his father changed the subject. "I need you to look into that human problem. The man who dared to capture your brother."

"Boar." He had been a leader of Sidney's former home, and a slaver. He'd escaped capture, but a battalion of dragons had been looking for him for weeks.

"Yes." The king nodded. "The trail is going cold, and the search unit needs a bit of encouragement. If they think you're on the case, perhaps they'll work harder to not be bested by the weakest of my sons."

Saber didn't recoil. His face didn't show a hint of the hurt that he felt. This barely counted as an insult coming from his father. "You want me to find him?"

His father scoffed. "As if you could. Go through the motions. Be enough of a nuisance to get them moving. You can do that well enough."

He wanted to slouch. Or cry. But he'd cried his last tears when he was eight years old, before his father could have them beaten out of him. "Of course, sir. I will be a nuisance."

"Irritate the true soldiers and keep your betrothed happy. Marry that dragon and do me proud." He waved his hand in dismissal.

An old instinct to defend himself reared inside of Saber, and he crushed it down. He stood and left his father with a bow. Yotar was waiting outside the door and entered as Saber left. He didn't flinch at the warm greeting his father gave the servant. It didn't even hurt anymore.

Saber didn't know why he was a perpetual disappointment to his father, and he knew he shouldn't care. Both Crux and Ranger had encouraged him to put the pain behind him.

If only that would work.

His father thought he couldn't even capture one weak human. A dragon child should have been able to handle the Boar person. Saber was more than capable. He didn't understand how Ranger had been captured. But he could capture the man.

That would show his father.

He stopped walking.

That *would* show his father. He'd been commanded to only be a nuisance, but he had *technically* been commanded to look for Boar. And if he succeeded, his father would have to acknowledge the success, wouldn't he? Saber would show up an elite unit and take down a person who had captured his older brother and tried to sell him into slavery.

He could do it. He had all of a soldier's training and more than enough determination.

He *would* do it.

He was ready to race off to find a ship to start his journey when his communicator beeped to remind him of a scheduled meeting with Lady Mirage. He was tempted to cancel, but if the marriage fell through, there was nothing he could do to escape his father's ire.

So instead, he typed up a message to a trusted dragon in the intelligence office asking for all data on Boar and to have a tracking algorithm prepared, and then he headed off to meet his betrothed.

Once he was through with an unpleasant and awkward teatime, he'd be off to meet his destiny.

4

———

That was the only conclusion Mirage could come to as she and Saber sat at a small table and sipped tea. There was a plate of cookies in front of them that neither had touched. She was eyeing a particularly jam-filled confection, but couldn't bring herself to do anything that might prolong this meeting.

Hopefully the cookies would still be there when her betrothed left.

He'd greeted her and asked after her parents. Then they'd been left alone. Well, mostly alone. Her mother was 'tending to her flowers' about thirty feet away at the edge of the garden maze. Mirage had never before seen her mother dig into the dirt, but apparently Saber bought the excuse.

Her mother couldn't hear them, but that didn't mean Mirage was safe from censure.

Mirage sipped her tea before it could get cold. Saber picked up his own cup and mirrored her movement.

How long until they could call this meeting a success and be done with it? Fifteen minutes? No, they would need to suffer at least an hour.

Was this what their marriage was going to be like? No discussion other than pleasantries. Awkward moments and long times apart.

She could walk away. She could tell Saber she wasn't marrying him and let that be that. It didn't matter that the king had set the date. She was a free citizen. She could make her own choices.

Then her family would be in disgrace with the king, and there would be dire consequences. She wasn't sure exactly *what* those consequences would be, but her mother's anxiety was nothing to ignore. She was afraid.

Mirage had to do her duty. There was no escaping it.

"Do you like to fly, your highness?" she asked, aiming for an innocuous topic they could speak on for hours. They were both dragons, after all.

"Please, call me Saber." Her betrothed sipped his tea again and then put the cup down. "And yes, I enjoy flying."

He didn't add more.

She didn't grit her teeth or make a sound of frustration, and she deserved an award for that. Instead she pressed on. "There's a lovely outlook not far from here. I often fly there to clear my head." He didn't seem likely to add more, so she kept up a monologue, talking about some of her favorite flying spots near her home.

She didn't speak of the more adventurous outings. Her mother would probably murder her if she heard about Mirage diving from the top of a waterfall in human form and transforming mid-air. Or the sky dances she'd done over an active volcano.

"Have you ever flown out past the Vemion Straits?" Saber asked. He seemed interested despite himself and leaned in towards her just a touch.

Mirage grinned at the memory he sparked. "Don't tell my mother. But I've been sneaking out there since I was thirteen." It was the first daring flight she had taken. Water in the straits whirred madly, and not even the most skilled swimmers tested them. But flying over them was a rite of passage. She'd tested herself over the roiling ocean, flying for almost an hour before realizing she had to turn back or risk falling into the water and drowning.

That opened up the conversation, and she and Saber spoke at length about some of their preferred flying paths. If there was anything most dragons could talk about at length, it was flight. Mirage was starting to feel optimistic, but once they ran out of places to talk about, their conversation subsided back into silence.

Great.

She felt every minute of the allotted hour tick by, and finally Saber made his excuses. "Thank you for your time, my lady. I enjoyed our conversation. We must do this again before the dedication ceremony." He kissed her hand and left.

Mirage's hand tingled and she looked down, as if she could see the impression of his lips, but there was no evidence. Of course there wouldn't be. She had to stop daydreaming.

Her mother sat down in the seat he'd vacated. "That seems to have gone well." She was overly optimistic, and she took the cookie Mirage had been eyeing and delicately bit into it.

Mirage didn't pout. "It went." She did not want to give her every detail, but would no doubt be forced to recall the event point by point before the day was done.

Her mother gave her a gentle smile. "You need to make an effort, my dear. You can't expect to fall in love over the course of one teatime."

"Who said anything about love?" Mirage wasn't about to put *that* kind of pressure on herself. Not with this arrangement. Love was a luxury for other people. She just wanted a husband she could tolerate.

"I do want you to be happy," her mother said, smile morphing into a frustrated expression. "And I think if you open yourself up to this, you will be. We chose you for Saber for a reason."

Mirage could have said something snarky right then, but she decided to keep her thoughts to herself. "I'm going to go wash up." She left her mother in the garden before she could be called back.

But instead of washing up, Mirage went for a walk. And she pondered her mother's words and the conversation with Saber.

They had no chance of getting to know each other if they could only meet in semi-chaperoned conditions under her mother's watchful eye. And if she could just *talk* to Saber, maybe she could see how he'd react to the truth about her. Maybe he'd want her anyway.

They needed to be able to talk like real people. But how could they do that?

Mirage took three running steps and jumped into the air, shifting into her dragon form and beating her wings to gain altitude before gravity could clutch her back into its domineering grasp. Maybe she and Saber could go on a flight together. They both liked flying. It was something to have in common.

If she said something to her mother about it, her

mother would insist on an entourage accompanying them across every mile.

No, thank you.

She needed to talk to Saber. And maybe tell him the truth. Or not. She couldn't decide. She hated the indecision, but this was her future she was talking about. If she said the wrong thing, she might ruin it all.

Her mother was paranoid, but she had good reason.

Mirage spotted him not long after she took to the air, and she flew even higher in the hopes that it wouldn't be obvious she was following him. Apparently, he was relying on his feet to get wherever he was going.

That question was answered only a few minutes later. He ended up in a shipyard. She circled around and watched him examine a small spaceship.

Was he going somewhere?

If he was going off planet for some time, she might lose her nerve when he got back. Her mother would doubtlessly whisper sweet poison in her ear and make her doubt herself and her memories. She needed to talk to him before he left, while her convictions were still fresh in her mind.

She dove back to the ground and shifted back to her human form. She found the ship he was on, but didn't see him anywhere. He must have already boarded.

"Saber? Are you around?" She didn't want to sneak up on him. But he didn't respond.

She found her way around the ship and saw that a large door was open. Apparently, if she wanted to talk to him, she was going to have to get on the damned ship herself.

She hoped he didn't think she was being too forward.

"Saber?" she asked as she slowly made her way up the gangplank and into what looked like a small cargo area.

She still didn't see him. He still didn't answer.

She hoped she had the right ship.

She walked from the cargo area into a small hallway and then heard something clank. She whipped around and saw through a window into the cargo area that the door to outside the ship had closed.

Mirage's heart thumped and she moved urgently, voice getting higher as she tried not to panic. "Saber!" She needed to find him before he took off.

She didn't know the layout of a ship like this. She had never been off the planet before. She sprinted up the central hallway, hoping it would lead to some kind of cockpit, but the ship jolted, and she fell flat on her back as it took off. She started sliding backwards and grabbed on to the bottom rung of a ladder which was bolted to the wall and held on for dear life.

They were rocketing toward space, and if Mirage survived this, her mother was going to kill her.

5

SABER LOVED the sensation of takeoff. There was something magnificent about feeling his body fight against the forces of gravity until the planet finally let go of him and he floated in space. He let his limbs rise up, free of the tyranny of their weight for only a few moments before engaging the antigravity drive. This wasn't a pleasure cruise. He didn't have time to enjoy all of the little quirks of space travel.

The intelligence report was in his hand. There was a hit on Boar not far from Vemion. If Saber could get there first, if he could beat his father's chosen recovery squad, he was sure to catch Boar and impress the king.

He hoped.

He had no idea how this one human was capable

of eluding dragons, but Boar's lucky streak was about to come to an end.

Saber gave it a week. By then he was going to have this guy in hand, and Boar was going to face dragon justice. The human could evade the hunt, but he wouldn't be able to evade flames.

He punched in the coordinates and sent a note of thanks off to his intelligence analyst. Now he just had to sit back and fly to a scarcely populated planet and hope Boar was easy to spot.

It was going to be easy.

That confidence lasted for all of three minutes. Then the alarm above the cockpit door sounded, and something pounded against it.

Saber let out a curse and jolted out of his seat. He looked at the security feed and saw that Lady Mirage was standing right outside the door.

How in the stars was she there?

He blinked a few times to make sure he wasn't seeing things, but it was definitely his betrothed. Even through the grainy security footage, he could see that she did not look happy.

Saber disengaged the lock, and she burst into the room.

"You have to turn the ship around right now!" She was spitting mad. Her hair had come out of its carefully constructed coiffure and dragon flame danced in her eyes.

And for some reason, her fury made his cock take attention. She was gorgeous in her anger. Saber was smart enough not to say it out loud. But it had him wondering if perhaps their impending marriage wouldn't be the cold, lifeless mistake he worried they were heading for.

"How did you get on here? Did you sneak aboard?" He ignored her demands in favor of his own. What was she doing here? He had done standard checks. Stowaways weren't exactly common, but it didn't mean that he didn't look out for them. He'd run a scan of life forms on the ship two minutes before closing the cargo door.

"You locked me in. I was just coming to talk. Now turn this ship around and take me home," Mirage demanded. Smoke started to emanate from her body, a sure sign of dragon anger.

She couldn't summon fire in her human form; a dragon needed to be fully shifted or in warrior form for that. And for that he was thankful. Fire on board a ship would doom them both.

And he wasn't about to give in. "I can't take you back home. I'm on a mission. And it's time sensitive." He didn't exactly want company on his journey to find Boar, but the man had a bad habit of moving fast. If Saber wasted time turning around and returning Mirage safely to her home, he was sure to lose out on this lead. Especially since he would have to explain himself to her rather demanding mother.

Even a prince had to answer for abduction, no matter how accidental.

"I am a lady," Mirage insisted, face full of fury. "You can't kidnap me. This is all a misunderstanding. It will take an hour at most. Take me home." The smoke was pouring off of her faster.

Saber wondered if maybe he was wrong about whether a person could manage to summon fire in their human form.

He shot out of his seat and stalked towards her. "You came on my ship. And I'm a prince. I can do whatever I want." He got up in her space and stared down at her, daring her to contradict him.

She glared. He expected her to slap him.

They were inches apart. He was tempted to kiss her. With all the life in her expression right now, he could see exactly what she would be like on the battlefield.

She might have had the hair and the dress of a lady, but there was a warrior inside of her straining to get out.

And he wanted to see what that warrior looked like when she was uncaged.

"You're really going to do this? Kidnap your betrothed like some ancient barbarian?" Her voice got quiet, dangerously quiet. Oh yes, violence was dancing close to the surface of his dragon bride.

There were old stories of barbarian kings kidnapping their brides and keeping them as plunder. Saber was starting to see the appeal. Would all that anger turn to passion?

"I will return you home," he promised. She started to smile in triumph before he continued. "In a few days. Feel free to contact your mother and let her know you're taking a trip. You're an adult. You can even tell her you're with me if you think she'll like that."

Mirage glared at him. "You're going to regret this."

"Just add it to my list." He'd regretted everything about this match so far. For some reason, he didn't see this making things worse.

Mirage glared before she spun on her heels and stalked out of the cockpit.

6

Mirage was no longer in danger of being bored by her fiancé. Infuriated? Sure. Enraged? Undoubtedly.

But bored? Not so much.

How *dare* he not allow her to return home?

Wasn't he supposed to check to make sure no one else was on the ship before taking off? He acted like it was her fault that his safety measures had been faulty. Like she *wanted* to jet off into space with him!

She wanted to go home.

Except… if she went home, her mother was going to have question upon question upon question. Questions Mirage didn't want to answer.

Her mother would wonder why Mirage had climbed aboard the ship in the first place. She would be horrified that Mirage had tried to speak to Saber alone. And she'd blame this entire blasted affair on Mirage.

The prince was above reproach.

Mirage slumped back against the hallway wall and banged her head back, satisfied by the metallic thump that echoed around her. She didn't want to answer those questions. She was sick of her mother's meddling.

And by staying with Saber, she would escape those questions. At least for a few days.

Her sour mood cleared as if it had never been there.

Mirage hadn't had this kind of freedom from her mother since… Well, she wasn't sure. Since her time at university?

Even then, her mother had been sure to contact her on a nearly daily basis to make certain she wasn't screwing up. Her time at school had been contingent upon good behavior, and Mirage had been sure to never step out of line.

This was the kind of adventure she lived for. At least in theory. Her biggest actual adventure to date involved a few daring flights. Right now, she could do something she'd never dreamed of. She could help a prince on his voyage to…

Where were they supposed to be going? Saber hadn't said. What was such a big deal that her fiancé couldn't turn around?

Now that she wasn't in such a bad mood, maybe she could find out.

Mirage headed back to the cockpit and found Saber sitting back down and studying a brightly lit screen.

"Where are we going?" she asked, no longer throwing accusations his way. She was ready to be of use. "And is there any way I can help?"

Saber punched something into the screen in front of him. His voice was firm. "I'm chasing a fugitive who's been engaging in the slave trade in our system. I need you to stay out of the way. This man is very dangerous." He didn't look up from his tablet.

"I'm not completely helpless," Mirage insisted. Now that she was here, she wanted to do something. "I'm a hell of a flyer. And I know how to use my fire."

"I don't doubt that." He finally looked up. His gaze flicked up and down, taking her in. She had the distinct feeling he found her wanting. "But you have no training. And I don't want you to be a liability." His expression softened. "I also don't want you to get hurt."

Mirage bristled. She was a dragon, well, half-dragon. She was tougher than she looked. And Saber should have known that.

But the best way to prove that she could be helpful was probably to listen to what he said. There was an open seat right beside him, so she sat down and strapped in. "So this is a dragon who's been selling slaves?" The practice was abhorrent. And illegal. The king didn't look kindly on slavers. She'd read accounts of just how viciously they were dealt with in the kingdom, and she approved. No one got to buy and sell people.

"He's human." Saber grimaced, and Mirage tried to hide her shock. "But he's wily. We've been after him for weeks." She thought he was going to leave it there, but then he kept speaking. "He caught my brother. Ranger escaped, but it takes a very clever human to capture a dragon prince."

Mirage had heard rumors that something like that happened to the middle son of the dragon king. But no one knew for sure how he had managed to find his human mate and come back to Vemion with hundreds of humans rescued from wherever they lived.

"What happened?" If anyone could tell her the true story, it was Saber.

"He—" Something beeped on one of the sensors and he broke off to look at it. Then he cursed. "There's a solar storm incoming."

"Is that a bad thing?" They were in space. How could a storm hurt them?

His jaw set. "We'll see."

He didn't tell her Ranger's story.

But Mirage eased back into her chair and watched

him work. It was interesting. He was no longer the polite dragon prince, but now seemed to be a competent pilot on a mission. She wasn't sure how much time had passed, probably an hour or two. She wasn't sure where they were going. She hoped that Saber would eventually tell her.

Then a warning light went off, and an alarm started beeping. She jolted, shocked at the sudden sound.

Saber started to move faster, poking at his instruments and making adjustments she didn't understand.

Then the ship shook, and Mirage's arms started to float of their own volition. That was the anti-grav failing. She didn't need to know much about ships to understand *that*.

"Hold tight!" Saber warned, voice teetering on the edge of panic. "That's the solar storm. We're in for a rough ride."

7

SABER ALMOST LOST control of the ship. He jerked it back, but it was a close thing. The solar storm was screwing with the instruments, and he didn't know if he and Mirage were going to get out of this thing alive.

He looked over at his would-be bride, but he couldn't spare the words for an apology or comfort. Maybe he should have turned around and taken her home when she asked. Neither of them would have been in this predicament then. The solar storm had come out of nowhere. He never would have flown in these conditions if it had been predicted.

But he also didn't have time for regrets.

They were nearing the planet that Boar was supposed to be on. But if the human got caught in the solar storm, it was likely he hadn't survived.

Saber put thoughts of the slaver out of his mind. They had to live through this before they could hunt the man down. The ship kept losing power, and he was using every trick he knew to keep the life support functioning while he brought them down to land.

As they hit the atmosphere, Saber prayed. The heat could burn them up, but he was sure he had the angle of entry right. The heat shield just had to do its job. And if they didn't die from the heat, the next challenge was reducing their rate of descent so that the impact didn't kill them.

Out of the corner of his eye, he saw Mirage gripping her armrests tight, with her eyes squeezed shut. She was handling it better than he expected. A normal person would've been screaming and praying. She was keeping her thoughts to herself.

He wasn't going to let her die.

The atmosphere released them, and Saber's bones felt heavy as gravity gripped them in its thrall. He engaged the mechanical wings of the ship so that they could glide as well as possible. It allowed them to decrease their velocity and still gave him a bit of control over where they might land.

The control panel in front of him was blinking and resetting at random. There wasn't much that he could do at this point other than manually steer the ship.

This planet wasn't inhabited, at least not well. Visitors from nearby in the system liked to come here to camp and test their hardiness on the rugged terrain. On the bright side, that meant that Saber wasn't likely to crash into any person or building.

Unfortunately, it also meant they weren't likely to find help.

They were coming in too fast, so he deployed the ship's parachutes. It was a last resort. It meant he'd lost most of the control given by the wings, and he wouldn't have much choice about where they landed.

But their velocity decreased slowly, and they floated down to the ground.

The landing wasn't easy. He jolted in his seat and Mirage grunted. But neither of them were hurt. At least not physically.

And by some miracle, they were both alive.

He still didn't turn to his betrothed. He smacked the dashboard in front of them a few times until one of the monitors turned back on. He punched in a distress call and targeted towards Vemion. If he was lucky, someone from home would hear it and send help their way.

But Saber didn't think they were lucky. Or rather, they had used up all of their luck in the landing.

"How are you feeling?" he asked Mirage. She had finally pried her hands off of the armrests of her chair, but she hadn't undone her safety harness.

She forced her lips into something that should've been a smile but instead looked like anything but. "Did you know this is my first time off planet?" She asked it lightly.

And if dry humor was what was keeping her going, Saber would do his best to match her tone. "The landings aren't usually as hard," he offered.

And that set her off laughing.

Saber joined in. The fear and nervousness of their fall all bubbled out of him, and by the time he'd breathed out his last laugh, he was starting to feel a little better.

They were alive. As long as they were alive, they could keep moving.

And maybe they would even find Boar. If *he* was alive.

"Do you think someone from home will come find us?" Mirage asked. "Where *are* we anyway?"

He named the planet, though she didn't seem to recognize it. "I sent out a distress call. But that solar storm is likely to interfere with our signals. There should be a ranger station somewhere on this planet. We'd do best to go find it. The terrain is unforgiving. Even the toughest of soldiers sometimes break on this planet."

Mirage took two deep breaths and then nodded. "Well, I was looking forward to a bit of time away from home. We might as well make the best of it."

Saber couldn't help but smile. His betrothed wasn't nearly as bad as he thought.

8

Mirage was afraid that if she stood up, her legs wouldn't hold her. The only reason she wasn't shaking was because her muscles were locked so tight they hurt. If she relaxed the slightest bit, she might end up screaming.

But she couldn't let Ranger see her falter. She was in it now, and she wasn't going to become a liability.

She'd never hear the end of it if she disappointed her dragon prince.

She breathed deep and wiggled her toes, slowly and consciously loosening every muscle from the ground up. It was a good reminder that they *were* on the ground. They'd survived the crash. She didn't need to panic.

Her lungs seized. Just because she didn't need to

panic didn't mean the panic wasn't threatening to take her over.

Saber already had the door to the cockpit open, and she could smell fresh air coming from somewhere. She forced herself out of her seat and took two swift steps before her body could realize what was happening. By then she was able to use momentum to keep moving.

Success.

Saber was on the ground by the time she made it out the door. He had his hands on his hips and was surveying the area. He'd shifted to his warrior form, his scales coming out to protect him from enemy fire, claws extending on his hands, and the suggestion of fangs glinting in his mouth.

Mirage shifted between one step and the next. If he thought there was danger, she wasn't going to be caught defenseless. Saber gave her an approving nod when she joined him.

She breathed deep, letting the fresh air fill her lungs. There were rolling hills in the distance covered in dense trees. The place was a green wonderland; it was difficult to believe no one had developed the planet.

In other circumstances, she may have loved this place.

Today she just wanted to go home.

"We need to find a place to set up camp," Saber

said. He turned back toward the ship and ducked into the cargo area. "There should be enough supplies for us to fashion a tent, and we certainly have enough food for at least a week… if you don't mind protein bars. The planet has plenty of water, so we won't lack for that. If we start hiking now, we can find a place to sleep by nightfall." He stuffed something in a pack and handed it to her.

Mirage took the pack and then realized what he was saying. "Are we heading toward a city? A port? What's your plan?"

He grimaced. "No cities here. If I can find us a map, maybe we'll locate a ranger's station. The sooner we leave, the sooner we can find it." He hitched his own pack over his shoulders.

"Wait, then why are we moving at all? The ship doesn't look too damaged, and it would make a great place to camp. We're protected from the elements, and if someone from home comes to find us, we'll be right here." Mirage had nothing against camping, but she wasn't about to give up a solid structure in favor of a flimsy bit of fabric.

Saber didn't agree. "We're moving because this planet attracts a certain kind of camper, the kind that likes to fight. And there might be a skilled slaver stalking around somewhere. Our only defensive option if we stay here is to seal up the ship and hope it holds. We'll be trapped. I'd prefer to be able to move. And since we have no tools to repair the ship, there's no point in sticking by it." He nodded towards the hills. "Let's go."

"Just like that?" Mirage wasn't about to move. "You said we have enough food for a week. The ship also has water. You're a *prince*. Surely someone will come looking for you in that time. Holing up doesn't sound so bad to me. We'll be defenseless out *there*."

"We're dragons, we're never defenseless." Smoke wafted off of him. The old proverb was true. A dragon couldn't hide his anger.

"Are you insisting we move because you truly think it's safer or because you want to catch this human and prove yourself?" She didn't know where that last bit came from, but from the way Saber scowled, it must have hit home.

He got close enough that the smoke coming off of him singed her nose. "We're moving."

Mirage was surprised that *her* skin hadn't started smoking. She didn't appreciate being treated like a child. She wasn't making her point out of stubbornness. It seemed ludicrous to abandon the ship.

But her prince was determined to be right.

They stared at each other. One of them was going to have to give in.

Saber's eyes flicked down to her lips and his

tongue swiped out to wet his own, drawing her attention to it.

Then their gazes locked again.

They were only a foot apart. It wouldn't take any effort to lean in and taste him.

He was her betrothed. They'd be sharing a lot more than kisses after their dedication ceremony. Before long, she'd know every secret his body held.

A little preview couldn't hurt.

She wanted to kiss him. Attraction ripped through her, and she wanted to clutch him close and seal her mouth against his. And she was fooling herself if she said it was because he was her betrothed.

He was a passionate man, one who held himself back because of the people around him. And she related to that so hard that it hurt.

Their match was supposed to be proper. They were supposed to follow the rules of society.

But they were a long way from society and its rules.

Did they dare to make their own?

She forced herself to take a step back. She wasn't going to kiss him just because he was sexy when he was angry. That road led to something destructive, and she wanted their relationship to be... well, she wasn't exactly sure what she could want from him.

But not anger.

She wasn't so greedy to demand or expect love, but she could at least ask for respect.

So she took another step back. "You've made your decision, your highness, let's go hiking."

He groaned and leaned forward before jerking back. "There's more to you than meets the eye, Lady Mirage. I plan to uncover your layers."

"That sounds like a threat," she said, but she had to hold back a smile as she said it.

He grinned, and she regretted not kissing him when she had the chance. "It's a promise."

9

Mirage trudged behind her stupid betrothed and glared at the mud that stuck to her shoes. It wasn't the mud's fault that her prince failed to see the wisdom of her idea. No, of course not. Why would they stay where they had real shelter when they could traipse off into the forest where they'd be at the mercy of whatever found them first?

She saw smoke coming off of her skin and made herself take a few deep breaths. She didn't want Saber to know that he had this much of an effect on her. He didn't. This was just frustration.

And frustrated arousal.

He'd almost kissed her. She'd almost kissed him.

Her body still ached for more.

But it wasn't going to happen. Especially if he

made her hike halfway across this world in search of a ranger station that may not exist.

"If you fume any harder, you're going to start a forest fire." Saber glanced back over his shoulder as he spoke.

Mirage glared. There was probably something she could say, but the words caught in her throat.

Saber showed his intelligence by turning back towards the path ahead of them and walking on. They walked for awhile. Mirage's feet hurt, there was mud between her toes, and the pack on her back was heavy.

"Why are we walking when we could fly?" she finally asked. They could cover so much more distance in the air. And there wouldn't be any mud.

"We've only gone a few miles. Hardly worth the shift. I wanted to get the lay of the land on foot. And…" he trailed off and refused to meet her eyes.

"And what?"

"I don't like carrying things while I'm flying. I feel like I'm going to drop them." His cheeks actually pinkened.

He was blushing?

"You could have asked me to carry the bags." She was trying very hard not to find his blush cute. She was angry at him, damn the stars, she wasn't trying to *like* him.

He looked very confused at that. "I think I see a good camping spot up ahead."

Mirage followed him, and when she saw the spot he was talking about, her mouth nearly dropped open.

It was paradise.

There was a lovely clearing full of grass and flowers, and a clear, bubbling stream that ran through the center. There was evidence of a firepit someone must have used at some point in the past, but it didn't make the place look tarnished.

She didn't want to admit Saber had a point about the camping. But she would have been sad to miss out on this place. "Did you know this was here?"

He shrugged and sat his bag down beside a fallen log. "This place exactly? No. But I figured something suitable must be."

She put her own bag down and rolled her shoulders. Her skirt was ripped near the hem, her shoes were a lost cause, and she looked like she'd spent a week in the wilderness, not a few hours. Her mother would have a heart attack if she saw her.

But Saber grinned when he looked up, and it warmed something inside of her.

"There's plenty of animals to hunt. How about I go find us something and you get the camp set up?" he asked.

"What makes you think I know how to set up

camp?" Mirage asked. "I can hunt for days, but when I camp out, I don't have a tent." She slammed her mouth shut when she realized what she'd admitted.

"Why do you look as if you've just admitted to murder?" Saber stood up and rolled his own shoulders. He clearly wasn't bothered by what she'd said.

"Because my mother would *rather* I admit to murder than an affinity for the outdoors." Mirage shuddered. She was never going to hear the end of this.

Saber took a step towards her. He kept doing that. Kept getting close. And he was either going to need to stop it or make good on the promise of his action. She wasn't sure which she wanted.

No, that was a lie.

She wanted his kiss almost as much as she wanted her next breath.

"You've said a lot about what your mother wants and what your mother expects. But she's not here right now. What do *you* want, Lady Mirage?" He gazed down at her, and the heat in her chest bubbled close to boiling.

She was breathing deep, chest heaving. She knew what she wanted, but she wasn't brave enough to say it. So she fell back to antagonism. "I want to hunt. You can pitch the tent."

"I thought you didn't need a tent," he challenged.

"I thought you didn't like carrying things in your dragon form." Why was she holding back a smile? Why did he make her feel *things?* "We could go together," she offered. "Two dragons are better than one."

"But you're a lady." He sounded more confused than critical.

"I'm a dragon first." She needed to get that through his skull. Dragon ladies didn't help anyone by pretending they weren't predators. "First to catch a goat wins!" She backed up to give herself enough room to shift.

And as she launched herself into the air, she was almost sure she heard Saber say, "I don't think we're going to find any goats."

She let the change overtake her and pumped her wings, flying high and free. She let out a cry and a small lick of flame. And a moment later, she was joined by a large black dragon with a flash of yellow scales under his wings.

A dragon she recognized.

This wasn't the first time flying with her prince.

And from the way he circled around her and sent a puff of smoke her way, he recognized her form too. They'd flown together months ago, a random meeting in the air that sent children below them cheering.

Mirage had been dreaming about that day ever

since it happened, and she'd felt regret that she'd never know who she was flying with.

Until now. When it turned out she was flying with her betrothed.

He sent a stream of fire her way and she deflected it, her own stream of fire somehow powerful enough to actually *bend* his flame. It defied the laws of physics, but at that moment Mirage didn't care. She was happy.

She and Saber danced in the sky. The planet might as well have belonged to them. They saw no one else. They heard no one else.

Not even goats.

But eventually they managed to scare up a bit of prey, and between flight and fire it didn't stand a chance. They ate in their dragon forms rather than deal with the mess that came with butchery for human digestion.

She would have flown all night, but eventually Saber led her back to their campground, where they shifted back to their human forms. Saber was looking at her like he'd never seen her before.

She couldn't stop smiling.

He took two strides forward and gathered her up in his arms, and then they were kissing and Mirage clung to him.

She hadn't realized it when she ran away, but she'd ended up exactly where she was meant to be.

10

SABER WAS THINKING with his cock. And his hands. And his lips. Stars knew he wasn't using his brain. It was too fried on lust and the taste of Mirage. He didn't want logic intruding with its stupid warnings and requirements.

He and Mirage were together. They were alive. And they flew together like they were meant to be.

That thought tugged at something in the back of his mind, but Saber ignored it too. Mirage overwhelmed his senses and Saber let himself be subsumed.

He almost wished he'd agreed to stay back at the crashed ship, only because the sleeping quarters were much more favorable than the forest floor. He wanted to get dirty, but not *that* way.

Though one of them must have been thinking

ahead. Somehow the fabric he'd brought to use as a makeshift tent was spread out on the ground, a useful bed.

He and Mirage stumbled back and ended up kneeling on the fabric, still caught up in each other and unable to pull back. But Saber forced himself into a moment of sense. Yes, Mirage was his betrothed. But she was still a lady. There were rules.

He tore his mouth away from her and almost dove right back in when he saw the way her hair was mussed, her eyes blown with desire. Her lips were swollen and wet, and he wanted nothing more than to take her back to his bed on Vemion and keep her there forever.

"Lady Mira—"

"I'm not an ignorant child, your highness. So think hard before you say anything." She put boldness to her words by stroking her fingers over his length.

Saber groaned. If he were a better man, he would have insisted on observing the proprieties. He hadn't absconded with his betrothed to have his way with her on an empty planet.

But now they were both breathing hard, lust hanging heavy in the air.

"Please tell me you're sure," he forced himself to ask. It would be torture to pull away now, but he would.

Somehow.

Instead, she leaned in and kissed him.

And that was the last Saber thought of pulling away.

His lady was all soft curves and wet kisses. And he was happy to lose himself in her. His cock strained against his trousers, and he wished he'd been smart enough to disrobe before they got started.

As her hips brushed against his, he rethought it. He'd already be buried deep inside of her without the barrier, and he didn't plan to end this anytime soon. Especially not until he had his betrothed writhing around him and wrung out with pleasure.

He made his way down her body, slowly undoing the laces over her dress and loosening the top as much as he could. It freed the tips of her breasts, and he paused to lay gentle kisses there, but her breasts weren't his goal.

Not now.

He'd save them for later.

He hiked up her skirt and grinned as she yanked the fabric higher, arching her hips to make it clear that she knew exactly what he planned and was in complete agreement.

The first taste of her killed him. It must have. Because nothing could taste so amazingly perfect. It wasn't just the taste of her. It was the way her skin moved under his tongue, the way she writhed and moaned and begged for more.

Saber would give her everything in the kingdom if only she asked.

But they were far away from the kingdom now, and on this planet they might have been the only two that existed. And what more could he want? He would have never known the blinding passion his betrothed could bring out in him. In herself. There'd never been a clue.

No need for clues now. Not when she was arching into him, her body rippling in pleasure as she cried out in orgasm.

This was what he was born to do. His only purpose was to bring her pleasure.

And to join her in it.

His cock strained against his pants, and he didn't know how he'd managed not to come. A warrior's discipline, surely. Because this was more of a challenge than any battle he'd ever fought.

He wanted to plunge inside of her and join her in pleasure. He wanted to bind them together in that intimate way.

But something held him back.

It wasn't a rejection of Mirage. Any thought of that was long gone. He'd reject his father's throne before he rejected her.

But they were far from home. And she was still a

lady. She was still owed certain things. Things he wanted to give her.

His hesitation must have shown. Mirage jerked at his waistband until his cock was freed and wrapped her hand around it. He groaned.

"What do you want, your highness?" She made his title sound like an erotic promise, and he'd be challenged not to get hard from those benign words. She stroked him again, and he almost lost the thread of his nerve.

But he managed to put his hand over hers and guide her. She tightened her grip until it was perfect, and the pace of her strokes nearly made his eyes cross.

He didn't last long, not when he was already riding the wave of *her* pleasure. And he came with her name on his lips.

She may have not been his choice of bride.

But he'd reject even his fated mate in favor of the woman in his arms.

Mirage wondered how she could convince Saber to stay on this barren planet alone with her forever. If the man she knew here was the one she was going to marry, she'd face the ceremony happily. But she feared the moment they stepped back on Vemion he'd revert to the distant man who could barely string a sentence together when they were forced to spend time with one another.

It would be a torture to bind her life to *that* man.

So how could he also be this one?

They were embarking on their third day on the planet, and Mirage knew that they couldn't stay here much longer. Solar storms didn't last forever. Eventually someone from home would come looking for them, or they would find one of the fabled rangers that patrolled this planet.

They weren't really alone.

Pity.

The soft sound of a footstep was her only warning before muscular arms wrapped around her and swooped her up in the air. Saber's lips brushed against her throat and made her stomach leap.

She could get so, *so* used to this. She already was, at least a little.

How would she survive if it went away?

"You look like you're thinking heavy thoughts," Saber said between kisses. "Why?"

If she were braver, she might have said something. It could even end up being a good thing if it meant they knew what they were to one another when this whole thing was over.

Instead she turned around and kissed him.

Kissing him was her new favorite thing. It overwhelmed her senses, and from the way Saber's body moved against her, he felt the same. She wanted everything from him, his life, his body, his heart. And she was determined to claim it while they were here.

Especially his body. She knew he was holding himself back from her. She just had to figure out why. And she had the sinking feeling it was out of some sense of propriety. And that wouldn't do.

But before she could move things forward, he

pulled back. She would have been disappointed if not for the playful glint in his eyes.

"Fly with me?" he asked.

Excitement surged through her. "Yes. Race you to the falls." She didn't wait for him to reply before turning around, leaping into the air, and shifting.

They'd discovered the waterfalls on their second day while hunting for a meal. It was a gorgeous landmark that was as big as a town, with water surging over cliffs so fast it almost tricked her eyes into thinking the water was flowing the wrong direction.

She was a fast flyer, but Saber was bigger, and he knew how to use his wingspan to his advantage.

A burst of heat on her flank was her only warning before Saber overtook her. She couldn't laugh in her dragon form, but the cry that tore out of her throat was joyful. And she paid Saber back in full by sending her own fire his way. It wasn't meant to hurt him. And if her flames licked him, it would only be a bit of warmth.

It took a lot of fire to harm a dragon.

She dived down and came up under him, nipping playfully at his vulnerable flank. In a real fight, he would have never allowed the move. But today wasn't about flying.

Saber took her by surprise when he executed a perfect spin and caught her up in his wings. His talons gripped her, just along the point of pain, and they began to plummet since neither one of them were flying.

She coughed a burst of smoke at him, and he released her.

This was what it was supposed to be like with her betrothed. She could grow to love him, she knew. If they could keep this joy. And in her dragon form, it was difficult to worry about any of the hardships that could come their way. There was only the flight and Saber.

They flew for a long time, exploring the planet and discovering its secrets. They didn't see any other people, though Mirage wasn't looking that hard. Other people could intrude on their happiness. And she just wanted to be alone with her...

Why did she almost think mate?

The thought almost startled her out of flight, but she recovered.

Saber wasn't her *mate*. She was starting to get excited about the thought of marrying him. But mate? No. Impossible.

It couldn't be.

Right?

She was afraid to hope. Mating was relatively rare. And to think it could happen in an arranged match was something out of the most fanciful daydream. She thought she could be happy with Saber. Wasn't that enough?

This was her problem. She didn't know how to be happy with what she had. She always wanted more, even when it didn't make any sense.

And she was ruining their flight.

He sent a puff of smoke her way as if to ask her if something was wrong. If they knew each other a bit better, he might have tried telepathy. But that only worked with dragons who knew one another very well.

And mates.

Had he tried and failed and discovered there was no bond between them?

Should *she* try?

She breathed fire in the hopes it would let some of the frustration out. And she didn't try to speak to him mind to mind. She didn't want confirmation that he wasn't her mate.

And she was even more scared of the possibility that he was.

She was a mess.

Mirage put it to the back of her mind. There was nothing more to think about. Saber wasn't her mate, and that was okay. She had never expected to find her mate before, so why should it be any different now?

And once the expectation was gone, she was able

to cast off her worries and have a good time. She and Saber played *pass the fireball*, a game every small dragon learned where they summoned fire and threw it back and forth between one another until it burned out. It required a deft hand with flame, and for some reason was easier with Saber than it had been with any other dragon.

Mirage was feeling a lot better by the time they started to fly back to their campsite. Maybe she could dare to hope that things would be fine once they returned to Vemion.

She was considering saying something to Saber.

But when they landed, it was clear something was wrong.

Their things were cast all around their site, and their bedding had been disturbed. Mirage smelled something foul and realized that someone had…

Was it an animal?

She didn't realize she'd said anything out loud until Saber placed a hand on her arm to hold her back. "I don't think so. This is deliberate. Stay behind me."

She wanted to protest, but Saber did have a warrior's training. For once, she was going to do as she was told.

"There." He pointed to a spot of mud several feet away from them. "Do you see that?"

She had to squint, and for a second, she thought

he was talking about a particularly gnarled stick. Then she saw what he meant.

"A shoeprint."

He shuddered, and her heart sank as he said, "I have a feeling Boar just found us."

At first, Saber wanted to capture Boar for the wrong he'd done to Ranger. Now he wanted to do him harm for daring to intrude on Saber's time with Mirage. Of course, there was no guarantee that the disturbance at their campsite was the work of the human slaver.

But Saber feared it was.

The place befouled deliberately. No animal would act like that. A human would. Especially a human like Boar, who had no respect for anyone but himself.

"Most of our things appear to be okay. I've gathered them off to the side." Mirage nodded to where she'd piled their packs. "What should we do?"

Saber should have never let his guard down. For a moment, he had forgotten his purpose in this mission. He'd let himself fall into the charm of his betrothed and care only about her. Why should he worry about Boar when he had a woman to seduce?

And he was a fool.

Boar could have struck at any moment.

They were lucky he'd only fouled their campsite.

This was why he hadn't wanted Mirage along on the mission. She was a liability. What if Boar found her alone? What if he hurt her?

Saber would make sure his end came swiftly and painfully.

"I need to track him." His mind was already on the hunt, and fire churned hot and wild inside of him. He wanted to unleash a breath of destruction. He'd burn this planet to the ground if it meant tracking down Boar.

"Perhaps you should investigate the campsite first," Mirage suggested quietly, resting one hand on his arm and turning him towards where they'd stayed the last two nights. "I wouldn't want you to get all worked up if this is really just some animals."

They'd have to move either way. It wasn't safe here anymore. They might have been dragons, but even dragons were vulnerable in their sleep.

"An animal that wears shoes?" But his betrothed was right. He needed to investigate closer. "Stay there," he told her. "There might be traps."

"I already—" She cut herself off with a sigh and stayed put.

She wanted to fight him on it, he was sure, but some protective instinct was riding close to the surface and he couldn't quite fight it. He needed to protect his ma—not mate. Of course not mate. She couldn't be.

But she was his woman, his responsibility. And he was going to return her to Vemion in one piece.

And then he'd wed her and take her to pieces in his bed.

Confident that Mirage would stay in one place, Saber searched the campsite for signs of who or what had disturbed them. There were a few predatory species that called the planet home, but most predators would be wise enough to stay away from dragons.

There was a deliberateness to the mess that suggested someone with the capacity for logic. The area where they'd slept was disturbed, along with their firepit. Every place they'd touched seemed to be touched by their interloper.

Saber breathed deep, but he didn't smell anything other than the existing mess. Then he caught a whiff of smoke.

"You're smoldering," Mirage warned from across the clearing.

Yes, he was. And he wanted to breathe fire. But he held it in and took several deep breaths until he was no longer smoking. It was fine. There was nothing more to be done about this.

Yet.

He circled back to Mirage, who had her arms crossed and a growing look of frustration on her face.

"Find any traps?" she asked, challenge lacing her words.

"Empty the bags." He wasn't going to waste time pandering to her mood, not when he was the warrior and she the lady.

"Don't command me like I'm a child," she snapped.

He bit back his response. Nothing good could come of it. "Please, Lady Mirage, first among all dragon females, empty the bags."

He expected a bit of fire, maybe some anger. He didn't know why she looked… scared. He would never hurt her, even if he wasn't betrothed to her. So what could make that look on her face? "Have no fear, Boar is no match for me."

Her expression cleared as if it had never been there at all. "I'm not scared of a *human*." There was, perhaps, more vehemence than was called for.

Saber did not understand this woman, but he looked forward to the day he would. He grabbed one of their bags and dumped it out.

"What are you doing?" It came out more shriek than question.

"Looking for trackers." He shifted through their things and felt a mix of violation and satisfaction when he found a small box with a flashing red light. He displayed it for Mirage. "He must be desperate to use something this obvious."

"Or he wants us to think we've found the only tracker so he can hunt us down," his betrothed suggested and upended the other bag. It only took her a few seconds to find another blinking flasher.

"Look for anything out of place." If he'd left two trackers, there was no telling what other presents he'd left behind.

They searched the bags, but there was nothing else that either of them could say didn't belong.

"Is that it?" Mirage asked.

Saber shrugged. "Seems like."

"I feel like we missed something." Her hand hovered over the things she'd searched.

Saber understood, but they couldn't stick around for much longer. "We need to find a place for you to stay while I search for Boar."

"Stay?" She jerked back. "*Stay?* I'm not going to stand to the side while you search. I am a *dragon*. Do not doubt me."

"I do not doubt you, my lady, but Boar is a dangerous man. He could harm you. He captured Ranger as if it were nothing." He didn't want to think about what Boar could do to Mirage. It stoked the fire inside of him until it threatened to rage into an inferno.

"Would you really stay here all day and argue while the trail goes cold? I'm coming with you. He's much less likely to snare me while I'm flying. You'd leave me vulnerable on the ground?" From the glint in her eye, she knew she'd landed a hit.

And she was right. She roused Saber's protective instincts, and he didn't want to take her anywhere danger might lurk. But she was a dragon. He'd flown with her and knew just how skilled she was in the air. Boar wouldn't be able to take her down without weapons.

But it still rankled. He still wanted to find a way to keep her safe.

On this planet, real safety didn't exist. And with Boar lurking, they were in even more danger.

"Fine. We hunt together. But stay near me. And you carry the bags." He turned away before he could glare at her triumphant grin.

This time, when they flew, it wasn't a joyful affair. There was no playing, no chasing, no fire. They cut through the air, crossing over their campsite and around the woods, looking for any evidence that it truly was Boar who had tampered with their campsite.

After a few minutes in the air, Mirage got his attention and gestured to a bit of rising smoke on the ground. They flew closer and saw the remnants of a campfire.

Boar's? No way to tell.

They stayed airborne for more than an hour, but there was no other sign of the human. If he was there, he was hiding in the dense woods, and the only way to find him would be on foot.

Saber didn't like the idea of sleeping where the slaver might be lurking, so he led Mirage to the foothills at the edge of the woods and found a sheltered place for them to sleep.

They shifted back, and Mirage sank down onto a rock. "It could have just been a wild animal," she said. "One of us could have left that shoeprint."

Saber wished he could agree, but he had a feeling they were about to face more danger than they were ready for.

13

MIRAGE WAS GOING to give herself away if she didn't get control of her emotions. And that would be disastrous. She didn't like the feeling of lying to her betrothed, but things were too precarious for the truth to come out now. He wasn't calling her abilities as a dragon into question.

He knew she could fly and use her fire.

He didn't know it was sheer luck and determination that made it possible.

It was true that most half-dragons could shift and fly and looked no different than full dragons. But enough favored their other half that it was a risk.

Mirage couldn't be human.

Her mother had pushed her hard, and she'd ended up shifting younger than most.

Saber knew nothing about that. No one knew of

her mother's indiscretion or Mirage's secret heritage. And he certainly wasn't going to find out before they returned to Vemion.

But as her feelings for him grew, she wasn't sure she could stand to keep the secret for much longer. She couldn't let him bind himself to her if he didn't know who she truly was.

Her mother's voice whispered poisonous words in her ear. She was who she was, and her heritage didn't matter. No one needed to know. Mirage didn't want to be known as the half-human freak, did she?

She shuddered.

"Are you cold?" Saber asked. He was tending to their small fire. An outcropping overhead protected them from the elements, so they'd used their tents as bedding instead of pitching them. It made the setup much easier.

"I'm fine," she insisted. She pushed all of her doubts and fears to the back of her mind. She wasn't going to give herself away after twenty-five years of keeping this secret. She was better than that. "You're adept at setting up a campsite," she observed. If they were talking, maybe her mind wouldn't get fixated on her personal problems.

Saber poked a stick into the fire to stoke it and then threw the stick on top of the weak flames. "I've been known to escape into the wilderness from time to time. Sometimes my dragon needs to roam."

An unexpected shard of longing ripped through her. Long flights free of interaction were one of her favorite things. She loved to let her dragon wings spread wide and feel the wind on her scales. "I normally sleep in my dragon skin when I'm outside. Not that I've had many chances." Her mother would rouse an army to chase her down if she knew, so Mirage only took chances when she was certain not to be caught.

"Would you prefer that tonight?" her betrothed asked. His clothes were a bit shabby from walking around, and it was the kind of humid that was unpleasant on human skin. There'd be no sticky sweat in dragon form.

But Mirage's eyes flicked up and down, taking him in. "This form has its advantages," she said.

His eyes narrowed, and it was his turn to look her up and down. She felt his gaze like a physical touch, and her body responded. The small fire was barely warm, but she felt as if she'd been scalded by a wave of heat.

"It will be warmer if we sleep beside one another," she managed to say in an even tone.

Saber was out of his seat in a flash and managed to knock her back gently into their bedding. Her legs went around his waist as their lips crashed together. She was already wet and wanting, and it wouldn't take much to bring her to the edge.

That he could do this to her with barely a touch, barely a kiss, let her know just how good of a match they could be. She'd been worried their bed would be cold. Now she wondered how many times they'd set it alight.

Literally.

Their clothes were a tangle as they wrestled them off, exchanging desperate kisses all the while. The reality of the day crashed into her. There was possibly a dangerous human out there who wouldn't hesitate to hurt them. This planet held other dangers. She and Saber could only rely on one another.

And that was just how she wanted it. She wanted this dragon prince at her side. She was falling so hard and fast that there was no way to slow it. And Mirage wasn't sure if she wanted to. What would it be like to love her husband?

How much would it hurt if he rejected her?

But she couldn't dream he would when he kissed her like this. When his hands roved over her body and brought her pleasure she'd never dreamed possible.

She loved the feel of Saber's flesh under her fingers. His muscles were hard and his skin was hot. And he was all hers.

There were no doubts about that when they were on a deserted planet. As for when they got home? Mirage's worries could begin again on Vemion.

Her fingers brushed against Saber's hard cock and he groaned. That noise sent a spike of pleasure through her. She wanted to feel him inside of her. He'd held back before, but not now. She needed him.

All of him.

His lips did wicked things to her, especially when he kissed his way down her body, past her breasts and belly, right to the core of her, where he feasted. Mirage couldn't hold her sounds back, and she didn't try as he worshipped her with his tongue.

How could a body feel so much pleasure?

What did she need to do to make it never end?

She writhed under his tongue and babbled out promises of forever. She might have been embarrassed in other circumstances, but not when her betrothed made her feel like this.

And when her pleasure crested, she gasped and called out his name.

Saber pulled back and wrapped his hand around his cock, stroking hard. But Mirage had just enough of her wits about her to ask for what she really wanted.

"Inside me, please." She was panting as she begged, and she didn't care.

Saber let out a ragged breath and his hand stilled on himself. "You deserve more than a ragged camp bed, my lady."

"I want *you*." She tugged his head down and kissed him fiercely. "Please. I need you."

With a groan, Saber surrendered to her kiss, and his body pressed hard against hers. She was sensitive, but she still needed more. She didn't know she could feel so empty.

Then his blunt head pressed against her entrance.

Oh.

Yes.

She liked that.

When he pushed inside of her, she breathed deep. She was full. Almost too full. And it hurt just a bit.

But Saber took it slow. He slid in inch by scant inch. And her body surrendered to his invasion and the pleasure he promised. He seated himself fully inside of her and they froze there, connected in the most primal way two beings could connect.

Saber looked down at her with a soft look on his face. She wanted to read more into it, but she was scared. What if she was wrong?

Then he started to move again, and her doubts were torn away on a wave of pleasure.

She moved with him, gripping tight as he took her body to its limits.

He found a spot inside of her that made her vision go white with pleasure, and then she was rippling around him as she came again, cresting through the pleasure.

He thrust again and came, emptying inside of her.

Mirage was going to need to do that with him again. A lot. She didn't think she'd ever get sick of her prince.

But as he pulled out of her and they got prepared for sleep, she wasn't sure how she'd ever manage to tell him the truth.

She'd given him her heart. And it wouldn't take much for him to break it.

14

SABER WAS FIDDLING with a piece of tech when Mirage blinked her eyes awake. The sun was hot, but not high overhead. It wasn't late in the day, not that time mattered much when they were marooned on the planet. She wanted to turn over and snuggle back under the covers. There was a weird sort of luxury to being stranded on a planet away from everyone they knew.

Saber let out a curse and threw the tech down into the dirt.

So much for extra sleep. Mirage threw the last bit of blanket off and pulled on her tattered clothes before crossing the campsite to get a better look at what Saber was doing. "What's that?" She nodded toward the innocuous piece of black metal he'd thrown on the ground.

He was starting to smoke in frustration, a plume forming around both of them. He took several deep breaths, and the smoke eventually dissipated.

"I snagged that communicator from the ship before we abandoned it," he said, glaring at the ground like it had insulted his mother. "I was hoping there was something wrong with it. Something I could fix. But it looks like the solar storm is what's keeping us from communicating."

Mirage picked up the communicator and handed it back to him after brushing off the dirt. "Well, if you throw it on the ground a few more times, it probably will be broken and then you can fix it," she offered with a smile.

He smiled back, but it was faint and faded to a look of concentration once he had the communicator back in hand. "I just wish we had some way to know if our distress beacon was picked up back home."

She sank down onto the log he was sitting on and leaned her head on his shoulder. It felt good to touch him. And her body warmed when he wrapped an arm around her and tugged her even closer so their bodies were flush against one another.

"Someone will come looking for us eventually. You know that." At first she had been worried, but she was really enjoying the freedom that the barren planet had to offer. No mother to badger her. No expectations. And a handsome prince all to herself. What more could she want?

"I'd happily spend weeks with you here," Saber admitted, turning to brush his lips against her forehead. "But not with the danger. If you get hurt…" he trailed off.

Not this again. "I can handle myself. I don't know how many times I have to say it." But she wasn't as offended as she'd been before, not now that she knew Saber better. At first she had thought that it was Saber thinking less of her, but that wasn't it at all.

He wanted to protect her. He wanted to keep her safe.

He didn't need to. But the thought that he wanted to made something warm settle in her chest.

He cared for her.

Saber didn't repeat that Boar was a threat specifically to her, and she was glad. She really could take care of herself. She didn't want to have a fight this morning. Especially not after last night.

"If there's no way to fix the communicator, maybe we can find another way to pass the time." Mirage ran her fingers up his arm and back down to clasp their hands together. But he didn't let her tug him toward their bedding. She tried not to pout. It was a struggle.

"You are temptation itself." Saber smiled. He lifted

their joined hands and kissed her fingers. "But we must stay on our guard."

Okay. Now they *had* to take care of Boar. She wasn't going to let that human ruin what time she had left alone with Saber. Who knew what her betrothed would be like when they got back to Vemion? If this was the only time she had with him like this, she wanted to cherish it.

"If the communicator isn't broken, how can we get the signal off the planet? How do we call home?" She didn't know much about tech, but two brains were better than one.

Saber hummed and thought before he answered. "This communicator probably has a fairly weak signal. If we can get it high up in the atmosphere that might be enough for it to get past the fluctuations caused by the solar storm and send the message home. But we have to get it pretty high."

"We have to get the *communicator* pretty high? Mountain high? Or wings high?" It sparked a bit of excitement in her. She had once flown so high that it felt like her wings were going to ice over and she wouldn't have enough air left to breathe.

But Mirage liked to push the boundaries of what she was capable of.

Saber dug into the pack beside his feet and pulled out a second small device. "This is a repeater. I'll have to fly high enough and then see if I can boost the signal from the ground." He seemed to be talking more to himself than to her.

And Mirage heard the issue in his plan immediately. "You can't fly it *and* boost the signal. Not unless you've been hiding even more talents from me." She smiled and nudged his shoulder, but he didn't smile back. "I can fly high. Give me the repeater. You work your magic on the communicator."

He didn't like it. That was clear from the look on his face. "That's dangerous. You should be the one on the ground."

They were really going to need to have a talk about what he considered dangerous. And for once, she was going to hope that logic would be enough to convince him of what needed to be done. "You're the one who understands the tech. I don't. But I can fly. You'll see me the entire time. I can do it."

He looked apprehensive, but after a minute, he handed her the repeater. "Give me a few minutes to get things set up. Then I need you to fly high." He leaned in and gave her a hard kiss.

Mirage chased it when he tried to pull away. She would much rather go back to bed than worry about getting a piece of faulty tech to function. But Saber tore himself away before things could get too hot, though the look he gave her was enough to make her shiver.

She had no idea how he marshaled the discipline to get back to work.

True to his word, it only took a few minutes until it was her turn to shift and grab the repeater before taking off and beating her wings as strong as she could, climbing nearly vertically into the air to try and find a signal that Saber could use.

The vertical climb strained her wings, and as the air got thinner, it got harder and harder to fly. She wasn't going to be able to maintain altitude for long. Especially as she realized she couldn't pull enough air into her lungs.

She forced herself to keep going. Even as her vision started to get blurry and her wings felt like they would ice over.

The repeater wasn't a communicator. And even if it was, she wouldn't be able to speak to Saber through her dragon throat. She wouldn't know if he was able to send the distress signal.

So she had to give him as much time as she could.

But after another few minutes, she had to descend. At a lower altitude, she could fly for longer, and she glided along the wind, finally able to breathe. She sent out a little puff of smoke to celebrate.

Then she saw movement down on the ground. At first she thought it was Saber trying to move to get a better signal. But Saber didn't move like that. And then she saw Saber was right where she had left him in the dense forest.

Was this Boar? The evil human Saber was supposed to be hunting?

Right now, it looked like the human was hunting *him*. She sent out a screech of warning, but she was sure that Saber didn't understand what she was trying to say.

She wished she could send a telepathic message to him. She wished they were mates. But she didn't even waste her energy in trying. She needed to get to him before Boar did. She wasn't going to let him get hurt.

She dove, heading towards the human, ready to end him with a burst of flame. But before she could summon her fire, the human lifted up something heavy looking and aimed it at her.

She only realized it was a laser rifle in the second before he shot a burst of energy at her and sent her crashing towards the ground.

15

Saber did everything he could to boost the distress signal. He knew that Mirage was flying high and that no dragon could sustain that altitude for long. It was too dangerous and taxing on the body. He couldn't let her hurt herself.

He wanted to watch her fly. She had the beauty and grace of an aerial dancer, but he had to focus on his equipment. They could dance in the sky later.

When he heard her shriek, his head jerked up, and he saw her in a warrior's dive, heading for something on the ground near him. It was a beautifully executed maneuver, but he had no idea why she was doing it.

He barely had a chance to think before he saw the blast of laser fire hit her and send her tumbling those final feet to the ground.

Something slammed into his chest, and it was as if *he* had been hit by the laser blast in addition to her.

He howled in rage, and his fire churned inside of him. He shifted into his warrior form and dropped the communicator to the ground, forgetting about trying to contact home and turning towards whatever danger stood near him on the ground.

The forest around him was dense, and there was no clear path, so he used his fire and his claws to make one.

But by the time he got to where Mirage had fallen, she was gone. The only sign of her were the drag marks that indicated that she must have switched back to her human form, and the footprints leading up to the small crater where she'd fallen.

Not just footprints. *Shoe* prints.

Definitely not an animal. Though that was a given, considering the laser blast. Not many animals could use lasers.

Saber followed the marks as far as he could. If he got his hands on Boar, the man would be dead in a second. But more than that, Saber was determined to find and save Mirage. She had risked herself for him. She must have seen Boar while she was descending, and she had tried to take the human out.

It wasn't her fault that the human was prepared for a dragon's attack.

Where had he learned that? Fire could only shoot

so far. And a laser rifle could usually shoot farther. It took guts, but a skilled human could shoot down a dragon in the middle of a dive. Something that Mirage clearly hadn't known.

But she wasn't a warrior. Why would she know that? No one shot dragons down back home.

He sped up as he followed the drag marks. Especially when he saw blood dripping on the ground. He was only a few minutes behind them. Boar would regret what he had done.

No, he wouldn't. He wouldn't have time to.

Saber knew he was supposed to capture the man. That was what his father wanted. That was what was expected of him. But Boar had made a mistake in capturing Mirage. And he would not live to make another one.

He came to a ravine when the drag marks stopped. It was just narrow enough that Saber could leap over it to get to the other side. But on the other side of the ravine, there were no drag marks. A small stream ran through the bottom of the ravine and that had to be where Boar had gone next.

Saber headed downstream in the hopes that that was the direction Boar had gone in. It was the only way that made sense if he was also carrying Mirage's weight. But finding the man had just gotten a lot more difficult.

It didn't matter. Saber would follow him to the

end of the earth. Because Mirage was his, and Boar would pay.

Mirage's whole body hurt, and her head felt like it was stuffed with fluff. She was lying on the hard ground and her hands were tied behind her back.

What was going on? What had happened to her?

She remembered flying. She remembered struggling against the thin air and trying to get the repeater high enough for Saber to get a message back home.

Had she succeeded?

Had she fallen?

If she had fallen, why were her hands tied together?

Then she remembered the flash of movement and the laser shot coming right for her.

Boar. He had shut her down, and wherever they were, he had her at his mercy.

A sharp boot kicked her in the stomach, and she groaned.

"You're awake. Finally. Took you long enough." The human's voice was gruff and mean. And he was foolish to get so close to a dragon. She reached for her fire. But in her human form, it was difficult to conjure. She couldn't even manage a puff of smoke.

Boar must've known what she was planning. He kicked her again and laughed. "I gave you a bit of something to take care of that. Stop the dragon from using their fire. Comes in handy. Of course it doesn't usually knock someone out. It knocks humans out. Wonder what that's about." He was looking at her with narrowed eyes, and Mirage wondered if he had somehow figured out her secret.

She couldn't breathe fire. But she could spit. And she did. This human deserved so much more than that. "Do you really think you're going to get off this planet alive?" she asked him through her scratchy voice.

"Once that prince of yours realizes the only way to get you back is to let me go, then yes. I am going to get off this planet." He kicked her again and backed up before she could ask more questions.

He was delusional. The second Saber figured out where they were, he was going to murder Boar, probably by burning the human to a crisp.

Mirage just had to survive until then.

It hurt to breathe. She worried that Boar had broken something, but she couldn't focus on that right now. She couldn't be a liability for when Saber came.

So she breathed deep and ignored the sharp pain in her stomach and summoned her warrior form.

She almost stopped in relief when she was able to shift. She couldn't summon her fire, but at least she had her claws.

Boar must not have noticed. Maybe he didn't know about the other form, maybe he didn't care about it. But at this point, it was Mirage's only weapon.

He had her bound with a vine of some kind, and Mirage was able to get the tip of her claw against the material. It took time, and she pricked her own wrists more than once, but she managed to free her arms.

She stayed lying on the ground. She didn't want Boar to realize that she could move.

Her arms burned, and she wanted to shake them out. It hurt. But she was afraid that if she made another move, Boar would use that laser rifle of his and take her out for good.

She wasn't going to die on this planet.

She could feel the fire deep in her chest. But every time she tried to reach for it, it was like there was a wall between her and her flame.

How long was this drug going to last?

Would she ever get her fire back?

What if this was forever?

That was a different kind of fear, one she wasn't sure she could face just yet.

Her whole life depended on being just as much of a dragon as anyone else. If she couldn't do what other dragons did, then she was nothing.

Tears threatened to fall, and Mirage buried them deep. She had plenty of practice doing that.

Saber, I don't know if you can hear me. But please come quick. They didn't have a telepathic connection. They weren't mates. That was just some vain hope, a childish dream that she had to let go. But maybe they knew each other well enough. Maybe Saber would hear her plea.

She had nothing else to lose. She kept sending the distress calls with her mind. She didn't hear any response from Saber. She didn't have much hope that he could hear.

How long had she been unconscious?

Where were they?

Her clothes were covered in dirt, as if she had been dragged a great distance, and some of the fabric was torn. That didn't just happen from the crash landing.

She heard footsteps, and Boar came closer. "I don't know where your little prince is, but it's time to give him a bit of motivation." He had the rifle resting on his shoulder, and there was a gleam in his eyes.

She didn't want him getting any closer.

She scrambled back, and her hands came apart.

"Tricky, tricky," Boar hissed. "You're going to learn not to disrespect me." He pointed the laser rifle right at her. "Don't try anything."

Her claws ached to tear into him, and the second he was close enough, she was going to make her move.

Then she heard a dragon screech as Saber flew by overhead, his shadow covering both of them.

Boar whipped around, pointing the laser rifle right at her betrothed. Mirage didn't think. She dove straight for Boar and wrestled for the gun. Her claws made it a bit difficult to grip, but she took grim satisfaction when she ripped into his skin.

But she wasn't a fighter, and Boar was. She got the gun out of his hands, but as she threw it to the side, he kicked her even harder in the stomach and sent her reeling back.

In the air, Saber screeched in rage.

She could feel the fire in the air before he let it loose, and it came out in a stream of energy heading right for Boar. Or, rather, right where Boar had been. He was going to miss, and Boar was sprinting for the rifle like his life depended on it, because it did.

On instinct, Mirage reached for Saber's fire and

redirected it, sending a burst of flame right at her captor.

He screamed and screamed and screamed.

And then he fell.

And then he was silent.

A moment later, Saber landed and shifted back to his human form. He looked at Boar long enough to make sure that the human was dead and not getting back up.

Then his gaze swung back to Mirage, and the intensity sent a different kind of heat through her.

He stopped close, and there was only one word on his lips. "Mate."

THE NEED TO claim Mirage in the most primal of ways was a fire raging inside of Saber. He wanted to lay her down right there and take her. She was his mate.

She was *his*.

But she was hurt.

There was a smudge of blood on her brow, and she was clutching her stomach like something was broken.

The need to claim changed into the need to care between one breath and the next. If Boar wasn't already dead, Saber would have cherished every moment he took in breaking the man apart.

But he was dead. His brother was avenged. The mission was over.

Now his mate was all that mattered.

She was staring at him, eyes wide and lips parted.

No god or devil could have stopped him from kissing her then. But he was gentle. He refused to add to her pain.

"You came for me," she said when he pulled back. She sounded surprised.

"I'll always come for you." He held her chin gently in his hands and was relieved to see the cut on her forehead was nothing more than a scratch. "What did he do to you? Are you hurt? I took the medkit from the ship. It's back with our things." If it were an option, he'd take all of her pain into himself. He didn't want her feeling a moment's discomfort.

"A few kicks, that's all. And it's not that bad. One shift, and I'll be good to go." She rested a hand on his arm. "Are we really…?"

"Can't you feel it?" The connection had been teasing him for days. He'd been so certain it wasn't possible that he'd rejected the thought rather than hope. "I heard you when I flew here."

Her hand tightened around his arm. "It's real."

"It's real. Let's leave this place. I'll come back and take a record of him, but you don't need to be here." He wanted to gather her up and fly with her in his arms, but she was just as much of a dragon as he was. "Can you shift?"

She nodded. "He gave me something that affects my fire, but I think so."

There was another crime Boar wouldn't pay for. The bastard.

But Mirage took two steps back and shifted before Saber could get too fired up. And he followed right behind her, staying close enough to help if she faltered.

She didn't.

And when they landed near their new campsite, she looked as good as new. The shift had helped to heal her, and she tipped her head back with a smile, breathing in the clean air.

Saber needed her.

Now.

His cock was an insistent throb in his pants. He wanted to tear his own clothes off with his claws, but that would take even more time than the other way. In a moment, he was naked, and when Mirage noticed, her eyes took him in and her smile turned carnal.

"My prince," she breathed.

"My mate." She was wearing too many clothes, and Saber was still in his warrior form. He tore her dress apart and pulled it off in seconds, baring her to his eyes and the air.

The sound she made was decadent, and he couldn't resist pulling her close and kissing her senseless. The taste of her was all he'd ever wanted. That and the feel of her skin pressed close against his.

How had he ever doubted what she was to him?

He was a fool.

But not any longer.

He clutched her close, her skin silken under his fingers. He wanted to run his hands over her all while holding her right *there*. He needed another arm. Anything that would allow him to bring her as much pleasure as a woman could feel.

She kissed him back, and he could taste the future. This was hope, destiny.

Perfect.

He needed inside her, but anything that would make him stop kissing her was torture, and he couldn't consider it. Not yet. Not until he'd had his fill.

His *temporary* fill. He knew he'd never have enough of her permanently.

Her body arched against his, and a wave of heat scalded through him. For a moment he thought it was a dragon's fire, but this was pure passion. Pure Mirage.

He laid her back on their hastily spread out bedding and reluctantly pulled back to get a good look at her. Her eyes were dark with pleasure and her chest heaved. She stared up at him in challenge, daring him to take her.

He'd take that dare. And any other challenge she threw his way.

He feasted on her, taking one of her stiff nipples into his mouth and rolling his tongue around until she moaned, the salty taste of her skin a balm to his soul. She writhed under him, and he knew he was doing something right. He wanted to capture the noises she made and hold them close to his heart.

He'd never be lonely again if he could only remember how she sounded.

His fingers found the wet heat between her legs and plunged in, feeling her heat engulf him. Her sounds became even more decadent, with unintelligible words interspersed. Was she making him promises? Did she even know what she was saying? He wanted to learn this secret language and give her *everything*.

His cock was an iron rod, and it took almost impossible effort to keep from plunging into her slick heat. But not yet, not until she was ready and begging for it. He was a warrior and a prince, he had the discipline to wait.

Even if it drove him mad.

This was his *mate* beneath him, the one woman in all of existence who belonged to him. He'd never expected to be blessed with her, and resisting for even a moment more was its own kind of torture.

But he persisted.

He kissed his way down her body until his head

was between her thighs and he could savor the most intimate taste of her.

She screamed his name and begged for more.

There was no longer any need to be quiet, to be cautious. They had one another and they were as safe as they were going to get. And he planned to take full advantage of that. He used his tongue and fingers like he was a trained pleasure slave, and it had Mirage digging her fingers into his hair and arching up against him.

He smiled against her in satisfaction. Yes, this was exactly what he wanted to give her.

This. And everything.

Her breath stuttered, and she gasped before she surrendered to his pleasurable onslaught. Then she was cresting, and he was right there to guide her through it, kissing and stroking and learning her every curve.

He'd die if he wasn't in her soon.

"Please, Saber, I need you," she said, clutching his arm and pulling him even closer.

She was his to command. And it was tortuous relief as he seated himself at her entrance and slid himself in. She was so tight around him that he feared this would be over all too soon, but he grabbed onto his discipline and held tight.

He was going to bring his mate more pleasure

than she could handle. And that meant controlling himself first.

He moved slowly, letting himself be gripped tight by her body. And then he was seated fully in her, joined to her as closely as two beings could be joined.

She was his mate. And he was never letting her go.

Something overtook him then, the passion getting to him, and he moved within her. Their bodies danced in unison, and Saber gave himself over to the pleasure of it. There was no time, no threat, nothing but the two of them bonded together.

He wanted this forever, and he was determined to have it. He would fight every battle, or give up all of his belongings, if it meant keeping Mirage as his mate.

And then she came again, her body gripping his cock. The sensation was too much and Saber let go, emptying himself inside of her as the pleasure ripped through him.

Yes, this was what he needed. For good.

He gathered her close in his arms, but after a moment, Mirage stiffened and pulled away. Then she turned toward him and met his gaze, eyes grim.

"There's something I need to tell you."

SHE MIGHT HAVE BEEN MAKING the biggest mistake of her life. Curled up in Saber's arms, Mirage knew she should let it drop.

But did she really know? Or were those just the fears that her mother had instilled in her over her entire life? Why was Mirage the one who had to hide when it was her mother's indiscretion?

"You're as stiff as a board." Saber held her closer. His skin smelled faintly of smoke in the way a dragon's should.

She turned her head and breathed deep, taking what comfort she could. If this was the last time he was going to hold her, she wanted it to last. "There's something I need to tell you," she said again, stronger this time.

"I'm listening." He sounded a bit apprehensive, but of course he would when she was acting so weird.

The words tried to stick in her throat, but she forced them out. "My father isn't my father. My mother had an affair shortly before their marriage. I'm half-human." It came out in a rush. It was the first time she'd ever said it out loud, and she felt like throwing up. Did confessions get easier over time?

She never wanted to say those words again.

Saber sat up straighter and loosened his hold on her, but he didn't let her go. "What do you mean?" he asked, as if it wasn't clear.

But she repeated herself. "My mother had a dalliance with a human man before she was married. She was pregnant with me when she married my father, and it's been a secret my whole life. I'm not a full-blooded dragon."

"I can see why you've kept this private." His voice was serious.

"Not private. Secret. Not even my brothers know. My father may suspect. But it's not something we speak of. Ever." Would her father still care for her if he knew the full truth?

"Do you want to tell everyone?" He still hadn't let her go.

"Stars, no!" The thought of it riled her stomach.

He turned so they were fully facing each other and pressed a gentle kiss to her forehead. "I will stand by you no matter what. You're my mate. And over these last few days I've grown to care for you more than I thought I ever could. Come home with me. Be my wife and my mate. Nothing else matters."

A wave of happiness crashed over her, and she threw her arms around Saber and tackled him backwards, kissing him senseless.

A long time later, they headed back to the ship. Boar no longer posed a threat, and if the message had gone through, then it was the most likely place a rescue ship would find them.

And that night, a small speeder landed just as Saber and Mirage were considering shifting to go for a hunt.

"I know that craft," Saber said as soon as he spotted it.

The hatch opened and Crux, Saber's oldest brother and the heir to the throne, stepped out. "You have caused mayhem, brother," was his greeting.

Saber tipped his head back and laughed. "No more than you."

Mirage shrank back. She hadn't exchanged more than a few words with Crux back on Vemion, and just his presence was enough to remind her of home in the worst way possible. Saber could care for her here, but would that hold true at home?

He turned her way and offered a bright smile before beckoning her back to him and then turning to his brother. "I have the best news."

"You do?" Crux didn't look convinced.

Saber put an arm around her shoulder. "Mirage is not just my betrothed. She's my mate. And I cannot wait to spend the rest of my life with her."

Crux's expression turned to glee, and he swept both of them up into a hug. "That *is* good news. You, me, and Ranger mated in the space of a month. That's a miracle."

If everyone reacted like Crux, Mirage had nothing to fear.

They packed up what they'd recovered and climbed into Crux's ship. She and Saber sat together in the back.

"You can spend time with your brother," she assured him. "I don't mind." She even felt brave for saying it.

"I've spent my life with my brother. I'll gladly take a few more hours alone with my mate."

But they didn't say much. All of the expectations of Vemion were starting to lay heavy on Mirage's shoulders. She was scared that she'd be torn away from Saber the second they got home.

She didn't voice her doubts. That would only make them stronger. But as they assailed her, she reached out and grabbed Saber's hand to remind her that they were in this together.

He was her mate, not just her betrothed.

So why did it feel like they were flying towards their doom?

19

Saber wanted to take Mirage straight to the palace with him and be done with the dedication ceremony. Why waste any more time on their betrothal when they were fated mates? As far as he was concerned, they were already bound as closely as a pair could be bound.

But Mirage needed to see her family. And Saber knew it would be better to deliver the news of his mating and Boar's demise in private.

And as for the news that Mirage was half-human? That would stay between them. Saber would stand by her if she wanted to tell the kingdom in the future. But he could understand why she wanted to keep it quiet.

There was a shift in the mood of the palace. And

it was confirmed when Saber was led immediately to his father after requesting an audience.

He couldn't remember the last time that had happened.

And when he entered his father's office, the king greeted him with a smile and an arm flung carelessly around his shoulders.

Had Saber entered into some parallel dimension?

"You've done me proud, son," said the king.

Yes, Saber was undoubtedly in a parallel dimension. But he'd enjoy it while he could.

"I'm glad I could do so. Boar was a blight, and now he will never harm another dragon. Or my—"

"About your betrothed," his father cut him off. "It's been reported that she snuck onto your ship in order to… well, there are *rumors*. And given the family history, the pairing was always a risk." He heaved a sigh. "I'd like to see all of my sons happily wed, but not at the expense of what's left of our legacy. You may end the betrothal. Find your own dragon lady. You have my blessing."

The air whooshed out of Saber like he'd been punched in the gut. "Family history?" he managed to stammer out. It had cost so much for Mirage to confess to the truth about her birth. Was it possible it wasn't as secret as she thought?

His father made a dismissive sound. "The dragonling uprising three centuries ago. Don't you know her family was on the side of the usurper? They denied it, of course, but they've been clawing their way out of that shame ever since."

Saber sagged in relief. And then he straightened. He didn't want his father to learn of anything else. "I thank you for giving me the choice, your highness. But I choose her."

The king blinked several times and opened his mouth to speak, but no words come out.

And this was the first time Saber could remember shocking his father silent. It didn't last for long. "You can't choose her! She's inappropriate."

"I don't care. She's my mate and I love her. I won't have anyone else." He didn't raise his voice. He wasn't arguing. In that moment, he was freer than he'd ever been before.

His father couldn't stop him. He may have been the king, but Saber had his own choice. And he could walk away from the family whenever he wanted. No one cared if the youngest son walked away. And with his two older brothers mated, it wasn't like he had much chance of inheriting anyway.

Thankfully.

And he didn't need to stick around and hear more about how he was a perpetual disappointment. He stood. "I'm marrying Lady Mirage, Father. Good day."

"Get back here now! I am your king!" His father sprung out of his seat to call him back.

But Saber was done listening. He had a mate to claim.

SABER PROVIDED transport back to her family's house, and Mirage was thankful. But she wished he was with her.

No. This was better. She had to stand on her own feet.

What could her mother actually do to her?

She'd spent most of her life living in fear of what would happen if someone found out the truth of her heritage. And now Saber knew. And he wanted her anyway. She was free. She was in love.

And she was no longer letting her mother get in her way.

The house seemed empty when she got there. No one came out to greet her, happy that she was safely home. No one yelled at her that she'd disgraced herself by disappearing.

No one cared at all.

She walked through the entrance and to the back of the house and into the atrium where her mother often spent her days. It was overgrown with greenery and flowers and smelled like home and secrets. This was where her mother told her the truth of her birth and insisted that she never tell a soul. This was the room that kept the family secrets.

As a matter of fact, she was fairly certain there was a centuries-old hidey-hole from a near-forgotten and completely failed uprising.

"Mother?" she called out when she didn't see her. She could hear someone moving around.

Then she turned a corner and saw her mother looking at flowers. She looked up at Mirage and took in her tattered dress and dirty skin.

Perhaps Mirage should have washed first.

Too late now.

"You let your prince see you like that?" her mother sneered. "Let me guess, he'll not have you now."

Mirage felt like she'd been slapped. It hurt so much she actually took a step back. She couldn't come up with an immediate reply.

Had her mother always spoken to her like this? Had she always allowed it?

Why?

"He knows the truth." She hadn't meant to say it, but she wanted to slap back.

Her mother jumped up, eyes wide and skin smoking. "You gave yourself away?"

"I told him." It felt so wrong to say it, but once the words were out, she started smiling. "I told him," she repeated. "And he still wants me. He understands that my birth isn't my fault. And that I shouldn't pay for anyone else's indiscretion." The words hit her mother again, and some of the color drained from her face.

"You think that now, when you've no doubt given yourself to him. When he sees you as a new plaything. But his love and trust will not last, little one. Prepare for the fall." She pulled her gardening gloves off and threw them to the ground.

Mirage could make excuses. She could tell her mother that Saber was her mate and that there was no question that things wouldn't end. Fate had brought them together. They didn't have to doubt.

She *could* say all that.

But why?

Her mother couldn't see it. Every time she looked at Mirage, she saw her own mistakes. Mirage was a risk that would never go away. The truth could come out at any time.

And the secret had been a prison of their own making.

Mirage refused to live inside of those walls any longer. And she certainly wasn't going to give away her chance at happiness to please her mother. She didn't need to make excuses. She didn't need to prove she was right.

She just needed to be happy.

Mirage smiled, and her mother looked at her like she'd grown a second head.

It didn't matter.

She turned and walked out of the atrium, ignoring her mother as she yelled for her to come back.

Mirage was done with her family. She had a new life to live.

For the first time in all her years, she didn't doubt. She had faith. Faith that what she felt for Saber was real. Faith in herself. Faith in him. And she wasn't going to let toxicity in to spoil it.

She was going to pack a bag and find a place to stay. It was time to get out of her house.

But before she could go up to her room, the front door burst open and Saber rushed in. He stopped short when he saw her. "You're here."

"Where else would I be?" She was already smiling. They'd only been apart a few hours and already he'd come for her.

He blinked a few times. "I'm not sure. I feared you'd be sent off to… where do they send people off to? Space colonies?"

She stepped closer, not quite touching him, but close enough that she could if she wanted. "Not even my mother could arrange that on such short notice."

"Did she welcome you back?" He understood the situation well enough not to look optimistic.

She shook her head. "No. She didn't. His highness?"

Saber shuddered. "He was proud that we took care of Boar. He was… not impressed with…"

"With me." She was sure there were rumors swirling, unless her mother had managed to hush up her disappearance. There were always rumors. "Do you care?"

"Not a bit. Come away with me." He held out a hand.

Mirage took it. "I thought you'd never ask."

20

THEY DID what dragons were meant to do. They flew. Mirage thought back to their first flight together when they had no idea who they were or who they'd become to one another. It had been joyous then.

It was even better now.

She left her worries for the future back on the ground. They could be dealt with later. She just wanted to fly with her mate.

And they *flew*.

Saber sped ahead, and it took most of her concentration to keep up. And when she shot ahead of him, she let out a lick of flame in the dragon version of a laugh. Then, just for fun, she sent that flame straight for Saber.

He redirected it harmlessly into the air above them, where it dissipated.

He was her *mate*. The evidence of it made her even happier.

It took Mirage a few minutes to realize where Saber was leading her. And when she did, she let out another burst of fire in joy.

The Vemion Straits.

She loved flying there. The swirling water was hypnotic in the ocean below, and the sudden drop between cliffs always took her breath away. It was a place she'd escaped to in secret for so long that going there with another person felt strange.

But only for a moment. Venturing there with her mate was its own kind of special.

They swooped through the strait, and Saber dived for the water. Mirage wasn't quite that brave. She watched as her mate dropped low and pulled up at the last moment, skimming his claws against the churning waves.

It was dangerous, but watching him inspired her, and she couldn't resist. She dived right after him, even faster than him. The water came up quickly, and she was scared she couldn't switch her path in time. But she managed a roll and some quick wing-work to save herself from plunging into the deadly water.

Saber was watching her. She didn't realize a dragon could look worried. But he didn't try to stop her. She had no doubt he'd dive in after her if she faltered, but he wanted to see what she could do.

With him at her side, she felt like she could do anything.

They flew through the strait for a long time. It was starting to get dark before either of them tired, but they silently agreed it was time to leave. The strait was dangerous during the day. At night it was deadly for even the most skilled flyer.

She wasn't sure where Saber was leading her. They flew back towards civilization and passed her family home without a backward glance. Mirage wondered if she'd ever go back.

That was silly. At the very least, she'd need to go back for her things.

But that house would never be her home again.

The cool evening air felt good against her scales, and as they left her old house behind them, a bit more of Mirage's worry fell away. She was exactly where she was supposed to be, flying at her mate's side, celebrating their survival and reveling in being a dragon.

Yes, a dragon. No need for qualifiers. No need to worry about someone finding out the truth. She wasn't lying. She was Lady Mirage, a dragon, and the mate of Prince Saber. Who cared about technicalities? He knew the truth, he accepted her.

That was enough.

She was enough.

Finally.

Mirage thought they were going to the castle. It was lit up like a chandelier in the darkening night. But Saber led them past the city and further into the darkness. There were foothills outside the city, and there were sprinklings of light as they passed by dwellings, but Mirage rarely flew this way. She much preferred flying over the ocean.

They skirted around the hills and over a lake, landing on the rocky shore on the edge of a forest. It was dark, but she could just make out a cabin protected by the dense canopy of trees.

"What is this place?" she asked once she shifted. She stretched her muscles. Despite the shift, she found she often cramped up if she didn't.

Saber was doing the same, but once he was done, he reached out and laced their fingers together, tugging her towards a path she could barely see. "This is my sanctuary."

"Aren't princes supposed to have castles?" she asked with a broad smile.

He laughed. "So you only want me for my castle?" He stopped, tugged her close, and covered her mouth with his own in a drugging kiss. "Are you sure about that?" he asked when he pulled back.

Mirage tried to remember what she'd just said, but her body was keyed up with want. "Huh?"

He laughed again, and they continued up the path. Once they neared the cabin, the lights turned on. They must have tripped a sensor, or it was keyed to Saber.

"When I'm here, I can just be myself," he said as they stood in front of the door. Now he looked a little nervous. "It isn't much."

"Are you nervous I'm going to hate your cabin?" That was crazy. Already Mirage loved it, and she hadn't seen the inside. But the setting was so perfect it could have been a bare hut and she would want to stay.

"I have another estate," he assured her, as if that mattered. "And use of any of the family castles. We don't have to make this our permanent residence."

That caught Mirage off guard for half a second, but she recovered before Saber noticed. Of course he was thinking about their future. Of course she would be living with him. Though their courtship hadn't been long, they'd been tried in fire. And they were mates.

What was the point of waiting?

Besides, she wasn't going back to her mother's house.

"Let me see your home, Saber," she said gently.

He opened the door.

The lights inside turned on slowly, the dimness brightening as she stepped inside, giving the place a dreamlike quality. There wasn't much to the cabin. As far as she could tell, it was almost all one big room, with a bathroom closed off for privacy.

Nothing like a normal prince would require.

But her prince was more than happy with this place.

"Did you build this place yourself?" She wouldn't be surprised. Saber was full of wonderful secrets, and she wanted to uncover them all.

He laughed. "Thank you for believing in me. But I can't say I possess the skill. I purchased it from an old dragon who liked to be alone. He wanted to move back to the city to be close to his grandchildren."

"Did he know he was selling to a prince?" She ran her finger over the rough wood of the interior wall.

"I don't think so. He would have named a much higher price if he knew." He nodded toward the kitchen area. "I keep this place stocked. Are you hungry?"

Though they'd flown all day, they hadn't hunted, and Mirage's stomach growled. "You can cook?"

He looked at her in affronted disbelief, "I cooked for you when we were stranded."

She raised an eyebrow. "On a campfire. And we did most of our eating in our dragon forms. What prince knows how to cook?"

"Your prince."

That made her stomach flip over. And she might have tugged him to the cozy looking bed in the corner if that same stomach hadn't growled at just that moment. "Okay, my prince, show me your culinary skills."

His expression told her he was taking up the challenge. He pulled out utensils and ingredients with enough confidence to assure her that he knew what he was doing. And she watched in fascination as he put together something that made her mouth water.

Then she took her first bite and couldn't hold back a moan.

"Make sounds like that and you won't finish the plate," he warned, eyes darkening with lust.

"You *can* cook," she said between bites. "Don't get any ideas about tearing me away from this plate before I've licked it clean."

The lust didn't go away, but he leaned back against the kitchen counter and ate from a plate of his own, watching her as she devoured his food. "I like providing for you," he admitted. "Will you let me?"

She finished the food and set her fork down. "If it involves more meals like that? Of course." She smiled, but then she grew serious. Because he wasn't only talking about food. And they had to both know where this match between them led. "I'm a dragon, my prince."

"Mate," he corrected. "Call me your mate."

"My *mate*. And I can hunt my own food and

provide for myself." He breathed in as if he were ready to argue, but she kept speaking. "But it would, perhaps, be nice to lean on someone from time to time. Someone who sees me as his equal."

"Yes, equals." He set their plates aside. "Always."

She smiled. "Good. Now let's test out that bed."

His gaze sharpened. "I love you." The words were an intimate connection. And then his lips were on hers, and Mirage surrendered to the pleasure that only her mate could give to her.

Two Months Later

"Drink your wine, brother," Crux commanded, nudging Saber in the shoulder and nodding to the goblet that was sitting on the table beside him.

"Did you poison it?" he asked reflexively. A younger brother always had to be on his guard.

"You think we'd do something like that to you?" Ranger asked from his other side.

"Of course." And now he was certain they'd done something to the wine.

"Well, if you're not going to drink it..." Ranger reached for it and gulped it down.

That was the other option. Big brothers, always stealing.

Saber heard the sound of his mate's laugh and smiled. They were at Ranger's estate in one of his vast gardens. He and his mate Sidney had made a home for themselves there in the last few months, and the humans they had rescued from Sidney's home settlement lived in a village not far away.

Crux and his mate, Courtney, lived in the main palace in Dragon City. Saber imagined that might be a nightmare with the king in residence, but the king had decided to tour the countryside for the next half-year, giving Crux and Courtney time alone.

And Saber and Mirage stayed at the lake cabin most days. Their wedding would be a spectacle, whenever they set the date, but for now they just wanted to enjoy their time together. Was dragon society a little scandalized? Perhaps.

Neither he nor Mirage cared.

"Let me try," he heard Sidney say to one of the other mates.

"Do you think father bribed the matchmaker?" Ranger mused.

"What? You went to the matchmaker?" Saber asked, as if he hadn't sat on her couch and listened to what she had to say.

"You're saying you didn't?" Crux demanded. "Though what she told me sounded like nonsense at the time."

"Same," Saber agreed. "I didn't need her advice to claim my mate."

"Because Father chose her for you," said Ranger with a teasing grin.

Saber glared. "At least I didn't let a *human* kidnap me."

"They lured me with a distress signal! I was fulfilling my duty." Ranger was indignant, but instead of doing anything to Saber, he just poured more wine.

"We went to the matchmaker on our own," said Saber. "Unless Father has suddenly gained hypnotic abilities, I doubt he influenced us to go."

They all shuddered at the thought of their father playing around in their minds.

"No more thinking of that," Crux commanded.

While Saber normally would do exactly the opposite of what his older brother said, just to spite him, he was content to follow this directive.

A high-pitched shriek went up from where their mates were clustered down the path, and Saber was out of his seat, running to see if Mirage was in danger. His brothers were right behind him.

But the only danger seemed to be coming from their mates themselves. Courtney and Mirage were both sprawled over Sidney, who had strange boots with wheels on her feet. She was laughing and massaging her knee.

"I need more practice," she said.

That made Courtney and Mirage laugh even harder.

"What's going on?" Crux demanded, looking at them with an expression that would make a young soldier cower in fear.

It made their mates cackle.

"I'm showing the girls my skates," Courtney explained once she got her laughter under control.

"You'll break her ankles!" From the look on his face, he was no fan of Courtney's fancy shoes.

"I can break my own ankles!" Sidney declared, rising to unsteady feet. She pushed one boot against the ground and glided towards Ranger. "I think I can fashion a pair of these for myself," she told her mate.

"Um…" Ranger's face went blank.

Saber laughed at his brothers.

Until Mirage spoke. "Can you make me a pair?"

Sidney's eyes lit up.

Saber rushed forward and put an arm around his mate. "I think we need to head home," he said, before the women could come up with any more crazy ideas.

"But we're—" she tried to say as he led her away.

He captured her mouth with a searing kiss, and when he pulled away, she was blinking, eyes dark with desire. "Yes, I think we should go home," she agreed. "It's been too long since I had you all to myself."

"It's been hours."

"As I said. Far too long. Want to race?" There was a gleam in her eye.

"What do I get if I win?" Already the need to jump into the air and take off was riding him.

She smiled. "Me."

"And what do you get if you win?" he had to ask. Though this was a game with no losers.

Her grin grew wild. "You. Taking me."

"You're on."

They sprinted and jumped into the air, shifting between forms like it was nothing. And as they raced home, Saber didn't care who won. He was with his mate. That was all that mattered.

Thank you for reading *Saber*!
I'd appreciate it so much if you would consider leaving a review.

INTERGALACTIC DATING AGENCY

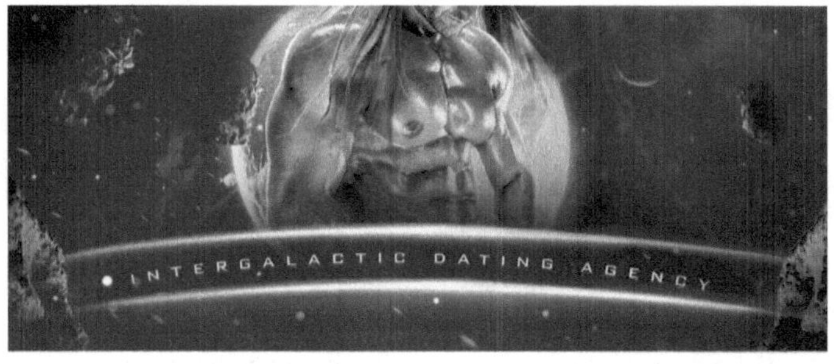

LOOKING for love that's out of this world? These strong, smart, sexy aliens are seeking mates from the Milky Way. Just hop onboard with your local Intergalactic Dating Agency. Join our group of authors as we explore the friendly skies and beyond with trilogies of cosmic craving, astral adventure, and otherworldly lovers. Warning: abductions may or may not be included!

WHAT'S TO READ NEXT: SYNNR'S
SAINT

Taken from Earth and used like a lab rat…

Emily was a normal law student until she was abducted by aliens. Forced to perform death defying feats by night and undergoing medical tests by day, she doesn't know how much longer she can take it. When one alien takes particular interest in her she's afraid things have gone from bad to worse. He's got wings and fangs, and he makes her heart pound. But she can't want an alien like that… can she?

He doesn't have time to rescue a human…

Oz is on Kilrym for a reason, and it's not to rescue the ethereal performer who captivates him by night. But covert ops are impossible when his mind is on the human who could be his fated mate. War is on the horizon, but what if the only way to save his people is to sacrifice Emily?

Despite the fact that they were born light years apart, they are a perfect match. But Oz is keeping secrets, and when Emily finds out the truth she may never be able to forgive him, no matter how much she needs him to survive and escape the planet alive.

Check it out!

and heroes abducted from Earth who find love – and wings! – with the alien warriors who rescue them.

Also available in audio!

Synnr's Saint

Synnr's Hope

Synnr's Spark

Synnr's Kiss

Guarded by the Shifter

Werewolf. Bodyguard. Mate.

The origins of these shifters are shrouded in mystery, but they're determined to protect their mates from any harm that comes their way.

Also available in audio!

Hunting Season

On the Prowl

Stalking Magic

Detyen Warriors

Detya was destroyed a hundred years ago. These

doomed warriors are out to find justice... and their mates.

The Detyen Warriors series brings you kick butt heroines, alpha alien heroes, fated mates, and relationships strong enough to span the galaxy!

The entire series is also available in audio!

Soulless

Ruthless

Heartless

Faultless

Endless

Alien Holiday Romance

Christmas... in space????

These alien holiday romances look beyond Earth's winter holidays and ring in the season across the galaxy! *Select titles available in audio.*

Snowed in with the Alien Beast

The Alien's Winter Gift

The Alien Reindeer's Wild Ride

Trapped with her Alien Mate

Alien Outlaws

Outlaws, schemes, and love… it's all there in the Alien Outlaws series…

Andie Munster is sick of life on Ixilta, the planet she got dumped on after being abducted from Earth six years ago. And when the mysterious and dangerous Xandr shows up looking for a way off the planet, she's half-prisoner, half-co-conspirator in a wild rush to escape.

Rogue Alien's Escape

Rogue Alien's Woman

Rogue Alien's Secret

Rogue Alien's Legacy

Mated to the Alien

Fated Mate Alien Romance

Detyens are doomed to die young if they don't find their fated mates.

Follow along as these mated pairs fight off aliens, corrupt dictators, prejudiced humans, pirates, and more! The books can be read or listened to in any order, though some characters show up in multiple stories.

Select books available in audio.

Pick a book and jump into the action today!

Ruwen

Tyral

Stoan

Cyborg

Krayter

Kayleb

Shayn

Braxtyn

Doryan

Dekon

Stealing the Alpha

The thief takes what she wants, but the alpha keeps what's his…

Join shifter thief Mel as she clashes with lion alpha Luke in an explosive trilogy of two opposites who can't keep away from one another.

Also available in audio!

The Alpha Heist

Entangled with the Thief

In the Alpha's Bed

Save with box sets!

Aliens. Shifters. Warriors. Mates. Get them all wrapped together in these special box sets. Save up to 30% off the price of buying the individual books, depending on the series!

Alien Outlaws: The Complete Series

Mated to the Alien Volume One (also available in audio)

Mated to the Alien Volume Two (also available in audio)

Mated to the Alien Volume Three

Mated to the Alien Volume Four

Stealing the Alpha: The Complete Series (also available in audio)

The Mate Bundle

Detyen Warriors Volume One (also available in audio)

Detyen Warriors Volume Two (also available in audio)

Zulir Warrior Mates Volume One (also available in audio)

Standalone Paranormal and Sci-Fi Romance:

Crashed

Mated on the Moon

Mated to the Alien Dragon

Marked

Bear in Mind

Alpha's Mercy

Gemma's Mate

Find more by Kate Rudolph at www.katerudolph.net

Kate Rudolph is a paranormal and alien romance author who lives in Indiana. She loves writing about kick butt heroines and the steamy heroes who love them. She's been devouring romance novels since she was too young to be reading them and had to hide her books so no one would take them away. She couldn't imagine a better job in this world than writing romances and sharing them with her fellow readers.

If you enjoyed this story, please consider leaving a review.